I0674498

A Most Scandalous Christmas

The Sins & Scandals Series

KELLY BOYCE

Copyright © 2016 Kelly Boyce

ISBN: 978-0-9948672-5-4

Editor: Nancy Cassidy

Cover design and Formatting: Kim Killion

This book is licensed for your personal enjoyment only. All rights reserved, including the right to reproduce this book, or a portion thereof, in any form. This book may not be resold or uploaded for distribution to others.

This is a work of fiction. Any references to historical events, real people, or real locales are used fictitiously. Other names, characters, places and incidents are the product of the author's imagination, and any resemblance to actual events, locales or persons, living or dead, is entirely coincidental.

THE SINS & SCANDALS SERIES

While there are those who spend their time in modest pursuits, upholding propriety befitting the lords and ladies of the ton, it would seem that for others scandal is just a sin away…

AN INVITATION TO SCANDAL
A SCANDALOUS PASSION
A SINFUL TEMPTATION
THE LADY'S SINFUL SECRET
SURRENDER TO SCANDAL
A SINNER NO MORE
THE SWEETEST SIN
A MOST SCANDALOUS CHRISTMAS
A HINT OF SCANDAL (Spring 2017)
SINS OF A SOLDIER (TBD)

DEDICATION

⸙

To my readers – may you find peace and happiness this holiday season and all the ones that follow.

CHAPTER ONE

This was an unmitigated disaster.

No. Correction. An unmitigated disaster would be a welcome respite from what this was.

This was Miss Patience Elmsley. Pressed against him in a most scandalous fashion, grasping onto his lapels for all she was worth, while his mother sat on her hind end not two feet away, staring up at him in abject horror.

Miss Elmsley removed her face from where she had tucked it into his neck, her warm breath and soft lips having found the narrow spot between where his cravat ended and his jawline began. Cold air moved swiftly in to replace the warmth, but he had little time to reconcile this as he found himself staring into a pair of crystal blue eyes that sparkled much like the newly fallen snow just outside the carriage that housed them.

"My goodness! What happened?" Miss Elmsley appeared more curious than upset, which was a far cry from his mother, who had already turned from shock to anger, her mouth pulled into a grim line of annoyance.

"I believe we may have thrown a wheel or some such thing." Why was she not moving? Her body had nestled itself rather boldly against his and there were certain parts of his that insisted in responding to this close proximity. If she did not remove herself with all due haste, he risked embarrassing them both. He diverted his attention in the hopes of alleviating such thoughts. "Mother, are you hurt?"

The tight lines of her mouth turned into an ugly scowl that did nothing to improve her disheveled appearance. He had been told that, once upon a time, she had been a very handsome woman, though it had faded over the decades. Likely the result of marriage to his father and the burden of all that came with that union.

She didn't bother answering his question, but rather issued a dictate, as was her way. "Might I suggest you release Miss Elmsley and see about the issue?"

Release Miss Elmsley? It was she who was clinging to him. But no, that wasn't quite right, was it? His arms twitched where he'd wrapped them around her, holding her in place. He let go immediately as if she were a hot coal and nearly unseated her. He grabbed her arms lest she land upon her rump next to his mother. Unfortunately, that brought them face to face. Nose to nose. Almost mouth to mouth and sweet heaven, say what you will about the young lady's reputation, but she had the most delectable—

Bloody hell! Miles swiftly set Miss Elmsley back into her seat and returned to his, taking in a deep breath to rid his senses of her delicate scent.

This entire day had been one trial after another. He should never have agreed to escort Miss Elmsley to Havelock Manor. What had he been thinking?

He reached down and helped his mother back to her seat next to Miss Elmsley, then reached for the handle on the door.

"Stay here." His order rang harsh in his ears but he cared not. His patience had worn thin. At least whatever had occurred to bring their journey to a halt allowed him a respite from being trapped inside with Miss Elmsley.

Or it would have, if she hadn't ignored his dictate and followed him out.

"Quite lovely, isn't it, Lord Walkerton?"

He turned and gave her an incredulous look. "Lovely?"

She stared out at the pristine vista while waving a hand toward the carriage. "The snow, I mean, not so much the broken wheel."

Miles looked down at the wheel, which did indeed have a damaged spoke. The driver had turned his attention to it now that the he'd calmed the horses.

Before he could answer, Miss Elmsley continued on. "The broken wheel is a bit of a bother. I had hoped to reach Havelock Manor before nightfall. But—" She shrugged then turned her gaze from the horizon to him and smiled.

Smiled!

Miles, in response, glared as politely as he could. This was hardly something to smile about. Did nothing faze her? Shouldn't she be ranting and raving? Crying? Something other than standing there smiling at him as if all was right with the world and matters such as broken wheels that left them stranded in the snow were hardly more than bumps in the road? Because this delay was not a bump in the road. It was a crater. An abyss of unfathomable depth.

Being stuck anywhere with a lady for whom scandalous behavior was akin to breathing was second only to death on things he'd currently like to avoid. Fine. Perhaps that was going a bit far. She had not, after all, ever been caught in a scandal, but given her pernicious and unpredictable behavior, it was only a matter of time. And he would very much prefer if he was nowhere in the near vicinity when that happened.

"Doubt I'll 'ave the wheel fixed in time, my lord," the driver said with a grave shake of his head. "I can truss it up 'nuff to get us to the nearest inn, but we'll 'ave to set up overnight to allow time to replace the wheel proper."

Miles expelled a long breath and resigned himself to his fate. "Very well. Do what you must, then take us to the nearest inn."

Once back in the carriage, Miss Elmsley addressed him, her usual smile twisted into an expression of annoyance. "I see no reason for you to have glared at me in such a manner, my lord. I merely commented upon the loveliness of the sunlight on the snow. Heavens, it isn't as if I am the one who broke the silly wheel and regardless, a brief delay is hardly the end of the world, is it?"

Her forthrightness never failed to shock him. Most young ladies would never dare point out the fact that a gentleman had glared at them. Then again, a proper gentleman would never glare at a young lady.

"Then might I ask your forgiveness for my momentary lapse in manners?"

"You are forgiven. Although, I might point out that perhaps you would have more success in finding yourself a bride if you were not so stern all the time. It's rather off-putting."

"I beg your pardon? Who said I was interested in finding a bride?" The words sputtered out of him. Her audacity stupefied him, though this appeared to have little effect on Miss Elmsley.

Instead, she gave him a knowing look, eyebrows raised, and eyes blinking innocently, a hint of sympathy—or was that pity—glinting in their depths. "Lady Rebecca? Hen?"

Miles scowled. The reminder of his failure to secure either of those two particular engagements stung. Both had ended after the ladies in question fell in love with men they preferred over him. Lady Rebecca to his half brother, Marcus Bowen, and the former Lady Henrietta to a future duke. A clear reminder of the uphill battle he faced in overcoming the ton's long memory of his late father's egregious sins. Appalling actions that continued to cast a dark stain over his family.

"I am quite certain my matrimonial state is none of your business."

His mother harrumphed in agreement. "I think you forget your place, Miss Elmsley."

Miss Elmsley turned her gaze away from Miles to land upon his mother. The sympathy she had bestowed upon him switched to sharpness, direct and unapologetic. Miss Elmsley may be a wisp of a thing, but she did not demure easily. "And which place might that be, Lady Walkerton?"

His mother's tart expression stiffened. She was unused to being questioned. Unused to a young lady who spoke up, asked questions, held opinions. "I find your behavior most unseemly. Though—" Mother sniffed. "I suppose that is to be expected when one takes your past behaviors into consideration."

Miss Elmsley's smile remained, but a brittle quality threaded around its edges. "I have done nothing in my past that I am ashamed of."

"You dumped a bowl of punch over Lady Susan's head." His mother straightened in her seat and puffed out her chest in victory.

"It was half a bowl of punch," Miss Elmsley corrected, "And she more than deserved it for the things she said and did to my cousin Judith."

"You made a spectacle of yourself." The way his mother stated this made it clear her opinion on the matter. That untoward behavior in a public forum was akin to death. "It is only a matter of time before you ruin yourself completely and then we shall see who has difficulty finding their way to the marital altar."

Some of the wind went out of Miss Elmsley's sails and something about the unexpected slump of her shoulders, the way the light dimmed and dulled in her bright blue eyes, drove Miles to action. Despite her forthrightness, Miss Elmsley did not deserve to be the target of his mother's caustic nature. A nature he had been subjected to for as far back as he could remember.

"Perhaps we will both have better luck over the holidays in finding suitable matches, Miss Elmsley."

Some of her verve returned. "Is that why you accepted the invitation to spend Christmas at Sheridan Park, my lord? To find yourself a bride?"

He should have known better than to think Miss Elmsley would leave the statement well enough alone.

"I am here to enjoy the holidays, nothing more. If something else comes of it, I will consider it a bonus. And if not, then so be it."

Which was a total and utter lie. Because he did need to find himself a wife. And not just any wife, but a well-bred, proper wife whose reputation was as pristine as the snow that currently surrounded them. A lady to whom scandal would never be attached. Perhaps if he could manage this, he could break free of his father's evil deeds. He could finally remove his mother to the dower house where her constant berating would no longer reach him. Nor would her accusing glare burn into him, a daily reminder that she blamed him for his inability to lift the family name from the gutter, instead of placing it upon the grave of the man truly responsible.

Miss Elmsley cocked her head to one side and studied him. It was a most disconcerting show of attention. Direct and unwavering it resulted in the uncomfortable sense that instead of looking at him, she looked into him. Miles shifted in his seat.

"How did you come by your invitation, if you don't mind me asking? I wasn't aware you held a close association with Lord and Lady Blackbourne, save for your courtship of his sister, Lady Rebecca, and given how that ended…" Her voice trailed off and ended in a shrug.

Miles cleared his throat. It was true that he and Lord Blackbourne had not formed a friendship. Blackbourne felt Miles had dragged the courtship on too long, a fact he could not dispute. Though, in his defense, it was Blackbourne's scandalous behavior that had necessitated his hesitancy in proposing to Lady Rebecca.

"I assure you, Lord Blackbourne and I have settled our past differences."

A situation that had come about by none other than Lady Rebecca's new husband, Mr. Marcus Bowen.

Miles's half brother.

Naturally, he left that little tidbit out. Save for a few individuals, Marcus's parentage, their relation, was a tightly guarded secret.

"Well, you needn't be so testy about it. I was merely making an observation."

"Must all your observations be made aloud?"

She twisted her pretty mouth to one side and looked at him as if he were an idiot. "It seems a bit redundant to make the observation to myself when I am already aware I think it. Observations are meant to be shared, do you not think so?"

"Not always, no."

"You're very easily riled, my lord. That, by the way, is another observation." And then she smiled and the sensation of it washed over him with surprising warmth, filling a space inside him he hadn't been aware of until that moment. Most unsettling, that.

Miles took a deep breath, allowing her smile to brush away his irritation. "Forgive me, Miss

Elmsley. I did not mean to be rude. I suppose the delay has me in a bit of a temper."

"Well, you shouldn't allow it to do so. We will arrive tomorrow and it is only a brief stopover. And you didn't tell me yet who issued your invitation."

He was beginning to realize very little swept past Miss Elmsley without her notice. While to some she may give the appearance of a flighty young lady, she was, in fact, just the opposite. She had a sharp mind, one that was unfortunately coupled with a quick tongue and bold manner.

"Mr. Marcus Bowen, if you must know."

She leaned forward in her seat and for a fleeting moment, the sensation of her falling into his arms as the carriage halted abruptly revisited him with a rush of heat. "Did he, indeed?"

"Yes." He took the conversation no further. While the idea of having a brother appealed to Miles greatly, it was not something he could speak of aloud, especially not to a chatterbox like Miss Elmsley, nor in the presence of his mother who considered the relationship between he and Marcus a personal insult.

Miles had been an only child, a lonely existence to be sure. Growing up, he had always wished for a brother. Having one would have made life much more palatable. The prospect of getting to know Marcus better appealed to him greatly.

And if Miles found a proper bride in the process, well, that would be the icing on the cake, so to speak. Little did he know then that accepting the invitation to Sheridan Park would come with the request that he and his mother escort Miss Elmsley to her family's estate, Havelock Manor, which shared a property line with Sheridan Park.

Escorting Miss Elmsley across a crowded ballroom, let alone all the way from London to the countryside, was an event fraught with peril. She had a way of attracting unwanted attention, with her outspoken nature and tendency toward impetuous behavior. But declining the request would cast him in a negative light, something he avoided at all costs.

And so, here he was. Stuck in a broken down carriage with a young woman who was far too chummy with scandal for his liking and only Mother to act as a buffer to keep things on the up and up. Though, thanks to the tincture she'd taken for her nerves, she had thus far spent most of their voyage sleeping, her snoring reverberating off the interior walls of the carriage. At least until the jolt of the broken wheel brought the sound to a merciful, albeit temporary, end.

"Well, I am very happy to hear there is no ill will between you and Lady Rebecca or Mr. Bowen. I find them both to be fine individuals, don't you agree?"

"He's a commoner," Miles's mother muttered, her disgust evident. "Her mother must have been horrified. Then again, the dowager countess married nothing more than a knight, so perhaps such predilections run in the family."

"I assure you there is nothing common about Mr. Bowen. And might I remind you that the dowager countess is married to my uncle." Miss Elmsley's tone cut sharp and a fire lit in her eyes at the slight to her family.

Before the conversation could devolve into battle of wills and words between the two women, Miles stepped in.

"I have heard nothing but praise spoken in regards to Sir Arran. A fine man, to be sure. I look forward to furthering our acquaintance."

Mercifully, the carriage jolted and their journey began to the nearest inn, where he would be forced to spend a night in close proximity to a sleeping Miss Elmsley.

A vision of her blonde curls spread out upon a pure white sheet teased his senses and he clenched his teeth to chase the image away.

To little effect.

"Oh, what a lovely inn. Quite charming. Don't you agree?" Patience said as Lord Walkerton assisted her down from the carriage. The driver had managed to repair the wheel to such a degree it carried them another few miles to the small village that housed The Burly Oak Inn. The ride had been a bumpy one that left her bones rattled and her bottom sore, but Patience refused to complain and give Lady Walkerton one more reason to look down at her. Besides, the bumpiness meant they were on their way once again. The sooner they arrived at their destination, the sooner she would be out from under Lady Walkerton's constant disapproving glare and Lord Walkerton's vigilant gaze. It was as if the man feared she might do something scandalous or untoward at any moment, and he would be held responsible.

"I shall reserve judgment until I am inside," Lord Walkerton said, releasing her hand the instant both her feet touched the ground. His tone indicated he did not hold out much hope in that regard. Hardly surprising. He appeared to look at everything with a skeptical eye. How exhausting that must be, always waiting for something to go wrong.

"Then you have not stayed here before, my lord?"

He turned his back to her and reached into the carriage for his mother, who had finally roused herself from her deep, snoring slumber. "I rarely have reason to travel out this way."

"Ah." Patience waited for more, but it appeared that was all Lord Walkerton deigned to say on the matter. "I see."

Conversing with the pompous earl proved an exhausting endeavor. Goodness, but was he always such a grumpy bear? How had Hen ever considered marriage to this man? Had she noticed, during their brief courtship, what a sour disposition he possessed? No wonder he had such difficulty in finding a bride, despite his lofty title. Not that she was one to talk. Her third Season loomed on the horizon with nary a hint of interest from any suitable gentleman. A fact her mother reminded her of with alarming regularity and a rather embarrassing degree of horror.

Regardless, there had to be at least one decent gentleman out there who would appreciate her special brand of…ah…what would we call it? Enthusiasm? Yes! That was the perfect word. She only needed to find that man—given he lived somewhere in the near vicinity—and all her problems would be solved. Mother could rest easy and Father would stop that sighing he did whenever she inadvertently caused some sort of brouhaha.

And she did want to marry and have a family of her own. Truly, she did. She just wanted to do so with the right person, like her cousin Judith had. Or Hen. They had married for love and both were deliriously happy with their new lives. Was it so much to ask for the same?

Patience glanced at Lord Walkerton. Perhaps she could use him as a sort of guideline. If she could find a gentleman who was Lord Walkerton's complete opposite—save for his appearance, as she really had nothing to criticize in that regard—then she would apply her charm and sway said gentleman into proposing to her. Lady Rebecca had indicated there would be a sufficient amount of eligible gentlemen attending the parties and events over the following weeks. Surely, she could find one that suited. Someone who would let her be who she was.

"Miss Elmsley?" The earl's stern tone interrupted her plotting.

"Yes?"

He moved his arm, indicating she should take it. "Shall we go inside?"

"Oh, yes! I am quite hungry. Do you think we are too late to take a meal?" The sun had set shortly after they were on their way again and the darkness left her disoriented and uncertain of the time of day. Though, her stomach rumbled as if it had been many hours since her last meal.

"Procuring rooms is the first order of business, Miss Elmsley," Lady Walkerton said, the countess's imperious voice cutting through the cold winter air like a shard of ice.

Easy for her to say. Likely, the earl's mother fed on fat little children that wandered too far into the forest. Patience bit her lip to hold back a smile at the image of the countess standing in the doorway of small, dilapidated cabin, attempting to entice wayward children to come hither. Any child in their right mind would take one look at her and run off at a fast gallop; head straight for home and never dare venture into the woods again.

"I will inquire upon supper with the innkeeper when I ask about rooms," Lord Walkerton said, his voice softening.

She looked up at him. He was taller than her by a head, broad of shoulder and trim of waist. She would bet a month's pin money he would be quite fetching in just his breeches and shirt. She covered her mouth with her gloved hand to hide the smile quivering on her lips. Lord Walkerton would faint dead away from shock if he knew she had pictured him in such a state of undress.

It was scandalous to think such thoughts, but some things could not be helped. Despite his irritable disposition, the earl was a strikingly handsome man, with his dark hair, hazel eyes, and sharp, imperious angles. His striking appearance couldn't help but invite wicked thoughts, and thoughts were perfectly acceptable, in her opinion, provided she didn't act upon them. Which she had no intention of doing.

As they entered The Burly Oak, the few patrons who sat about the main room glanced in their direction. Their gazes scraped over Patience in that way some men had that made her feel as if she were standing in nothing but her shift. She moved a little closer to Lord Walkerton and in response he shot the men one of his infamous glares, prompting them to return to their previous conversation.

The scent from the kitchen rushed out to greet them. Patience breathed deeply. Beef stew, if she wasn't mistaken. Her stomach gnawed with hunger.

"Oh my, but doesn't that smell divine?" Despite her small stature, she had been cursed with a rather voracious appetite. Not very ladylike, but not one of her worst attributes, surely. Cook rather appreciated it, at least.

Lord Walkerton left them for a moment to speak to the proprietor of the establishment and procure them rooms and meals, leaving her alone with his mother.

"Are you enjoying our trip, Lady Walkerton?"

"Not particularly, no." The woman was only a couple of inches taller than Patience, but she used her superior height to look down her broad nose in a condescending manner that irked.

"And why is that?"

"I find such travel tedious and unnecessary."

"I see. You would have preferred to stay in London, then?" Patience would have preferred that Lady Walkerton had stayed behind as well. Her company was rather taxing and impossible to enjoy.

"Yes. I see no point in this excursion."

Patience twisted her mouth to one side. It was not difficult to see where her son inherited his tetchy nature. She had heard the late Lord Walkerton had been quite convivial in comparison.

Of course, she had heard other things about the man as well.

Darker, more disturbing things.

Lord Walkerton returned a moment later, breaking the strained silence that had grown between Patience and the countess. When he addressed them, his gaze did little more than skim over the top of Patience's head, as if she was not worthy of his direct attention. The slight hurt and though she attempted to brush it away, a bruised residue remained.

"The innkeeper has prepared a private area where we might dine and I have procured two rooms for our stay. Mother, you and Miss Elmsley will share, of course. The trunks will be brought up to our rooms while we take our meal. This way." He swept an arm toward a short hallway.

His mother took possession of Lord Walkerton's free arm, then fixed her nose in the air as she prepared to head toward the succulent scent of beef wafting up to greet them, leaving Patience on her own.

When she did not immediately move, she received another stern glance from Lord Walkerton. "Is there a problem, Miss Elmsley?"

She forced a smile. Her ability to maintain a cheerful demeanor had been sorely tested by this journey. How she longed to reach Havelock Manor and join in the festivities of the Season and be surrounded by people who did not hold themselves in such high esteem that they had forgotten how to smile or enjoy themselves.

"No, my lord. No problem at all."

CHAPTER TWO

To say sharing a room with Lady Walkerton had been an enjoyable affair would be a bold-faced lie. Anyone who observed the dark circles beneath Patience's eyes this morning or witnessed the way the corners of her mouth drooped would know so. As if Lady Walkerton's dour personality had not been enough to contend with, she'd been forced to share a bed with the lady and risk being deafened by her incessant snoring. Even burrowing beneath the pillow had done little to mitigate the ungodly noise.

"Are you not well, Miss Elmsley? You look rather pallid this morning. It is not very fetching. I hope you are not falling ill. I would hate to have my son and I catch something that would ruin our holidays."

How very thoughtful of Lady Walkerton to inform Patience, between bites of ham and biscuits, of what she already knew. Breakfast today was the type of hearty fare that she would normally be pleased to find on the table, but this morning she barely had the energy to lift her fork.

"I'm afraid I did not sleep well, my lady."

"Hmph. Nor did I. Horribly uncomfortable beds. Why, I barely slept a wink. But what can one expect from such a lowly establishment?"

Patience raised her eyebrows. The Burly Oak Inn was a perfectly comfortable establishment and given the uninterrupted snoring, it was clear Lady Walkerton had slept like the dead. Except for the fact the dead did not make anywhere near as much noise. Rather than point this out, she smiled. Or attempted to, at least. In the end, all she managed was a bit of a twitch in her right cheek.

Lord Walkerton entered the room; his presence filling it in a rather disquieting way. His mother had indicated he'd had taken his meal earlier, and then gone to the stable to assess the status of the repairs to the carriage. He glanced down at her plate as he took his seat. "You are not eating, Miss Elmsley."

Given he had issued a statement, rather than an inquiry, she answered in kind. "No, my lord. I am not."

"Is the meal not to your liking?"

"I am certain it is fine. I am simply too tired to partake in it, I'm afraid."

"You did not sleep well?"

His powers of deduction amazed. "No, I did not." She glanced toward his mother, who paid her little heed as she devoured her breakfast in a way that bordered the edge of polite table manners. Her distaste of The Burly Oak obviously did not extend to its hearty fare.

Lord Walkerton's gaze followed hers then returned to rest upon Patience. Understanding dawned in his hazel eyes, warming them to a degree she found quite pleasing. "Ah. I see. Very well then.

Well, we should be good to leave once your meal is done. The trunks are being loaded onto the carriage as we speak. Provided we encounter no further hindrances, we should reach Havelock Manor before nightfall."

"Splendid." Patience did her best to find the positive side of things, but this morning, she struggled. The beautiful sunshine of yesterday had given way to dark gray clouds that hung low in the sky and the prospect of spending another day in a bumpy carriage listening to Lady Walkerton's snoring and attempting conversation with the aloof earl did nothing to improve her mood.

She lifted a bite of ham to her mouth and forced herself to eat at least a little. She would need all her strength to see her to the end of this trip.

The Miss Elmsley who had traveled with them yesterday was nowhere in evidence this morning as the carriage pulled away from The Burly Oak. Miles had to admit he missed her. The sullen, silent version that had taken her place reminded him of a lit fuse that had unexpectedly fizzled out. What had caused such a turnabout?

A mercurial sort, obviously. Miles did not care for such. He preferred companions of a steadier, dependable nature. That way, you always knew what you were in for and there were no surprises. He loathed surprises. He'd had enough of those growing up with his father, a man who had possessed his own unpredictable disposition. Jovial and entertaining one minute, surly and prone to violence the next. Thankfully, the late earl spent little time at home.

His father had never explained his long absences, but rumors abounded. Horrible truths that finally came to light shortly before his death. Women he had violated and tossed aside as if they were nothing more than playthings for his amusement. It was one of those women who had finally ended his father's life.

And at Sheridan Park, no less.

Miles let out a weary breath and leaned his head against the plush squabs of the carriage to stare up at the ceiling. Was it any wonder Mother had not wanted to come here? Not that there had been any love lost between his parents. They had married for title and position and all but despised each other for the duration of their marriage.

Was that what he could expect as well?

"You are doing an unusual amount of sighing, my lord."

Miles returned his gaze to Miss Elmsley. She had issued her statement without looking at him, the view out the window obviously more to her liking. With her posture erect and her hands folded primly in her lap she looked the very picture of a demure young lady. Though the picture deceived, as the hint of a frown that rested upon her pretty face indicated unhappiness. A state he had not witnessed in her before.

This change in demeanor left him oddly disturbed and with the unsettling need to rectify it.

"And how much sighing signifies as an unusual amount?" he asked.

She glanced over at him without moving her head, her light blue eyes skimming across his countenance like the soft brush of fingertips against his skin. There and then gone once her attention returned to the landscape beyond the window, but its effect lingered in a most unexpected way and in the most bothersome of places.

"The amount you are doing. I would not have taken you for a sigher."

"And what do you take me as, Miss Elmsley?" Why had he asked such a question? What did it matter? And yet, curiosity filled him and he held his breath awaiting her answer.

"Stuffy. Priggish, I suppose."

Stuffy? Priggish? Was it any surprise curiosity had killed the cat? He should have never posed the question, especially to a woman known for speaking her mind without censure.

Her description of him filled him with dissatisfaction. Is that how everyone saw him? Yes, he was a stickler for proper behavior, but what choice did he have? Mother had harped on him since he was in short pants that it was the only way to distance themselves from his father's behavior. Achieving this distance was the one thing that informed all of his decisions, his actions. It was his only hope in ensuring the ton did not look upon him as if at any moment he might begin to exhibit predilections reminiscent of his father's.

If he did not act impeccably, the sullied reputation his father had left their family with would never fade. The burden of changing people's perception weighed heavily upon his shoulders, a yoke he had carried for as long as he could remember.

"How lovely," he muttered. "You could not have lied and said I was handsome and dashing?"

Her gaze left the window and turned to meet his. "You are quite handsome, my lord. Everyone thinks so."

Her words were spoken plainly and with no artifice or coquettish batting of her lashes to add any other meaning than to state a simple fact. He should be pleased she thought him handsome, but her easy admission lacked any feeling and left him instead aching for something more.

"I suppose that is something, though I still have my, what did you call it?—ah yes, priggishness—to contend with." He started to sigh then caught himself, swallowing the sound as he searched for other topics to converse upon in the hopes of bringing back the lively companion of yesterday. "Do you have any particular plans for the holidays aside from attending a slew of parties and such?"

Miss Elmsley scratched at the tip of her nose just below where a light smattering of freckles dotted the bridge. "I expect Mother is hoping I will find a husband over the holidays. I have been told there will be any number of eligible gentlemen of suitable qualifications at the festivities Lord and Lady Blackbourne are hosting."

She sounded less than pleased by this notion. Peculiar. Wasn't that what every lady wished for? A suitable match that led to marriage and a family?

"And you do not wish to find such a gentleman?"

Her narrow shoulders drooped. She was a slight thing, fine-boned and wispy, yet he could not claim she appeared weak. If anything, a spritely energy pulsated from within her, giving the appearance of inner strength and fortitude. The dichotomy was rather perplexing.

Miss Elmsley re-folded her hands neatly upon her lap. "I have no objections to a husband, my lord. I would very much like to marry and have a family, but I would prefer to find a gentleman who suits me as I am, not a gentleman who expects me to spend my life being proper and pious and pretty and perfect."

"That's quite a list, Miss Elmsley. Are you quite certain that is what most gentlemen want?"

One golden eyebrow arched upward. "Is that not what you are looking for, my lord?"

Her question took him aback, but he answered nonetheless. "I would be happy with proper. If she were pretty, that would be welcome as well. As for pious or perfect, I do not claim a strong tie to either of those things and therefore would not expect them of my chosen wife."

"So all you require is a proper wife? Nothing more?"

"Pleasant would be a nice addition."

"Proper and pleasant then." She pulled a face that echoed her next thought on the subject. "Sounds like a recipe for a very boring existence."

Her bluntness never failed to shock. Most ladies would have smiled and said, *how lovely*, wished him well in his pursuits and left it at that. Then again, he was not conversing with most ladies. He was conversing with Miss Elmsley, for whom the notion of propriety was a nebulous idea at best. With a propensity for being outspoken when silence might have been a superior choice, or in motion when stillness was better called for, she operated on a level all her own, eschewing proper etiquette whenever she deemed it unnecessary.

Unfortunately, she deemed it unnecessary quite often.

He cleared his throat. "It is clear then, that my idea of a happy life and yours are unlikely to ever cross paths."

"*Very* unlikely. What of love and laughter and silliness and fun? Do you not wish for any of those things?"

Love would be nice. The thought raced through his head with alarming speed, startling and unwanted. He did not expect love. He wasn't even certain he would recognize the emotion if it presented itself. Love was not something he had witnessed during his childhood, nor had he been introduced to it in adulthood. He had felt a strong affection for Lady Rebecca during their courtship, and he had been fond of Lady Henrietta, but had he loved them? No. At least he didn't think so. As for the other items on her list—

"I do not see how silliness and fun factor into a successful marriage."

Miss Elmsley's lovely features arranged themselves to form a picture of surprise and—was that revulsion? "You don't see? But...how... How can you not?" She shook her head, looking at him as if he had crawled out from under a bridge, hunchbacked and covered in warts.

The carriage went over a bump, jostling them and interrupting his mother's snoring for a brief moment before she settled in once again, giving Miles time to form his answer. Except, the harder he thought on it, the more it dawned on him that he did not *have* a suitable answer and the one he gave made him sound, well, stuffy and priggish.

"Our sort does not marry for such trivial matters."

Miss Elmsley shook her head and looked at him with pity. "Then I feel very sorry for *your sort*, Lord Walkerton. Very sorry indeed."

CHAPTER THREE

Relief rushed through Patience as the carriage she shared with Lord Walkerton and his mother made its way up the long drive and stopped in front of Havelock Manor. Despite loving the hectic swirl of London, the site of Havelock Manor always filled her with a sense of home in a way the townhouse in the city never did. Though Elmsdale was her father's countryseat, it was her mother's family home, Havelock, with its wild landscape and relaxed nature that suited her much better.

Her mother rushed down the steps to greet her and pulled Patience into a tight hug, barely giving Lord Walkerton time to release her hand after assisting her from the carriage. Yes, it was good to be with family again.

"Good heavens, I wondered what had happened to you, my dear. You were set to arrive yesterday! Did something transpire to keep you away?" Her mother's gaze bounced between Patience and Lord Walkerton, but not before Patience noted a hopeful gleam in her mother's eye. She pressed her lips together and swallowed the groan that threatened to escape.

"Forgive our tardiness, my lady," Lord Walkerton said. "We ran into a spot of trouble with a broken wheel and had to put up for the night. My apologies for any concern this might have caused."

"Oh, Lord Walkerton, I have no doubt my daughter was in the best of hands. I thank you and your mother for taking such good care of my dear girl." Her mother leaned in a bit closer to the earl and lowered her voice. "I know she can be a bit of a handful at times."

"Mother!"

"What?"

"I am not *a handful*. I am merely—" What?

"Exuberant?" Lord Walkerton offered, his eyes crinkling ever so slightly in the corners, as if he'd amused himself with his contribution to the conversation.

Patience glared, then turned to her mother. "And you wouldn't have had to worry if you hadn't insisted on leaving me behind in London for a fortnight with Cousin Fiona."

Mother shot her an indignant look and pulled at the wool shawl she had tossed over her shoulders before running out of the house. "My dear, you know I had to come home and help with the preparations for the festive ball being thrown two days hence."

"I am certain Gloria and Abigail have the matter well in hand, Mother." Patience's Uncle Arran had married the Dowager Countess of Blackbourne the Christmas before. Given that previous to this, Gloria had managed more than her fair share of illustrious events at Sheridan Park, the idea that the great lady, or her daughter-in-law, the current Lady

Blackbourne, required any assistance was a bit absurd.

Mother brushed away her suggestion. "Another set of hands never spoiled the broth. Of course, you will be in attendance, Lord Walkerton."

The earl executed an abbreviated bow in answer, though whether he was pleased with his attendance or not, Patience could not tell. He was not the most readable of men.

"Mother and I look forward to the festivities with great anticipation, Lady Elmsley."

"And where is your mother, my lord?"

"Sleeping," Patience cut in. *Please, for all that was holy, do not wake the beast.* She could not countenance another moment of that woman's sour disposition. The fact that she had slept for most of the trip, despite the consequence of the horrid snoring that came of it, was a godsend, in Patience's estimation.

"Traveling exhausts her," Lord Walkerton added.

Mother peered inside the carriage, where Lady Walkerton had yet to awaken. "Ah, I see."

"Well, I should continue on. They are expecting us at Sheridan Park and I'm certain Mother will wish to continue her slumber in a proper bed." Lord Walkerton smiled in full this time, as if he had just told the wittiest joke. And while he hadn't, it hardly mattered as Patience was transfixed by the change such an expression brought to his handsome, if rather austere, features.

The weight of seriousness that always gave him the appearance of solemnity, bled away, replaced by an unexpected lightness. His eyes once again crinkled in their corners and his lips stretched to

reveal an even set of teeth and—heaven forbid—
Lord Walkerton had a dimple in his left cheek! Did
others know about this? Patience couldn't help but
feel as if she had just discovered a tightly held
secret, one she did not wish to keep, but, save for
Mother, there was no one else present to share it
with. Oh, where was Hen or Judith when she
needed them? Or even Charlie, though likely he
would be less impressed.

"Has my wayward brother returned yet,
Mother?" She and Charlie were hardly ever out of
each other's company for long. Mostly because
their mother insisted her older brother keep a sharp
eye on her to ensure she did not step out of bounds,
but also because the two siblings enjoyed each
other's company. Charlie was one of the few men of
her acquaintance she could be herself around
without worrying about causing offense or shocking
him out of his Hessians by saying or doing
something just a wee bit outside the bounds of
propriety.

"He has promised to arrive before nightfall, my
dear, and I have no doubt he will do just that."

Patience gave her mother a look. Charlie was
many things, but punctual had never been one of
them.

"Speaking of arrivals, I should bid adieu and be
on my way," Lord Walkerton said.

"It is a shame you must leave so soon, my lord."
Her mother stepped forward, her hands clasped
against her belly, the hopeful gleam back in her eye.
"Are you certain you and Lady Walkerton cannot
join us for tea?"

Patience could have told Mother not to bother. Likely Lord Walkerton could not wait to relieve himself of her presence.

"I thank you for the invitation, but as we were expected yesterday, I should likely not delay. I wouldn't want to cause anyone any concern over our absence."

"Very well then. We shall see you soon in the whirlwind of activities planned for the forthcoming weeks."

Lord Walkerton bowed. "I look forward to it, Lady Elmsley. Miss Elmsley, I thank you for your company during our journey. It was most…entertaining."

He offered up a polite smile, though it looked nothing like the one from only a moment ago that had left her transfixed. Pity. She would have enjoyed seeing his dimple one last time, given the rarity of such an event. Something about that smile gave her hope that hidden somewhere beneath all of his proper decorum, he possessed the smallest bit of happiness waiting to burst forth. She didn't know why that was important to her, but it was. Though serious and stern, she did not think Lord Walkerton an unkind man. Misguided in his opinions, yes, but not unkind. Therefore, he deserved to find happiness.

Whether he wanted to or not, well, that was another matter altogether.

As Miles was ushered into the grand hall of the main house of Sheridan Park, his arrival proved a far different event than the one he'd witnessed when delivering Miss Elmsley to Havelock Manor. While Lady Blackbourne gave every indication of being happy for his arrival, no one rushed out to greet him before he even made his way up the steps. There was no loved one to offer a warm embrace. No indication that his absence had been noted or that any emptiness had been filled upon his return.

Not that he expected Lady Blackbourne to do such. Why, they barely knew each other. Her entrance into Society had been brusquely interrupted by the scandal surrounding her uncle's death, leaving her family shunned by all for a time. Still, the disparity in his greeting was rather noticeable and brought home to roost the fact that he had never received that particular kind of a welcome home from anyone at anytime, regardless of how long he had been gone.

His mother had never taken much interest in his comings and goings. His father had rarely been around for most of Miles's life and when he was, Miles had done his best to avoid him. If his father noticed, he had not cared enough to comment.

What was it like to be greeted in the way Lady Elmsley had her daughter? Rushing out and wrapping her arms around her daughter as if she had been gone a year and not the fortnight that had framed her absence? And why was it that the more Miles replayed the scene in his mind, the deeper the ache he experienced in his chest? It was pure foolishness, that's what it was. Brought on by too much time listening to Miss Elmsley and her insistence that a proper life should never get in the way of a happy life.

A dangerous way of thinking if ever there was one. It set one up for disappointment. How could it not? It was just that kind of thinking that had likely brought Miss Patience Elmsley to the edge of ruination one too many times.

Patience. He rolled the name over on his tongue. Had her parents known that quality would be the one thing they would need the most with their daughter, even at the time of her birth? A sudden laugh escaped Miles and drew a sharp scowl from his mother as they made their way down the hallway to their assigned rooms. He quickly hid the sound under a quick throat clearing, the unexpected laughter surprising him as much as it had annoyed his mother.

"Lady Walkerton, this is your room. I hope it is to your liking," Lady Blackbourne stopped and opened the door to one of the bedchambers, interrupting Miles's thoughts. Just as well. They had taken a dangerous turn. Thoughts of Miss Elmsley had a way of tangling his mind into knots. She perplexed him with her opinions with respect to happiness, as if it was a state easily attained. That had never been his experience, and yet it appeared to be second nature to her.

His mother stood inside the well-appointed room and glanced around, her expression grim. Miles had not noticed how truly miserable his mother was until he'd spent two days with her sitting next to Miss Elmsley. The comparison had been rather troubling. Was he like that as well? Miserable and thorny, always seeing the worst in situations instead of the possibilities?

Stuffy and priggish.

Her descriptors settled like a stone in his stomach.

"Thank you, Lady Blackbourne. This will do, I suppose."

Miles cringed at his mother's rather inhospitable remark, but Lady Blackbourne remained unaffected.

"Then I shall leave you to get settled. Shall I send up a tray of tea and a light lunch? I'm certain you will wish to rest after your long trip."

"Yes, thank you. Such unnecessary travel during this time of year has left me uncommonly exhausted. If you might send up my lady's maid, I would appreciate it. I assume our servants arrived on time?" Mother sent Miles a disparaging look. He had sent his valet and Mother's lady's maid on ahead of their own carriage by several hours while he finished a few business matters before their departure. Had they left at the same time, he might have switched out the carriages with the servants and allowed them to arrive on time, instead of taking a night at The Burly Oak. Though, doubtless, Mother would have found disfavor in arriving in a carriage of lesser quality had that been the case.

"They have arrived safe and sound," Lady Blackbourne stated and walked farther into the room to pull the rope next to the bed. "I shall leave you to settle in while I show Lord Walkerton to his accommodations. Good day."

Miles followed Lady Blackbourne up the hallway farther in silence until it opened into an atria with large windows on one side and portraits of past Earls of Blackbourne lining the wall opposite them. By then, the silence had begun to wear on him.

"I should apologize for my mother's rather brusque manner, my lady. She does not take to travel well."

The countess smiled. "I suppose it must be a bit awkward for her coming here given what happened to her husband, as well as the relationship between you and Marcus."

Lady Blackbourne was one of a few select individuals privy to the fact that Miles and Marcus Bowen shared a paternal connection. That was the only reference Marcus would use in reference to the man who had sired them both. Given the circumstances of Marcus's conception and the tragedies that ensued as a result, Miles did not blame him.

"I cannot say if she finds it awkward. She does not speak of my father and prefers to carry on as if any relationship between me and Mr. Bowen simply does not exist," Miles said.

Lady Blackbourne turned to him, her blue eyes sharp and assessing. "But you do not share those feelings?"

Miles was unaccustomed to speaking to someone he barely knew about such delicate or personal matters, but he had the sense Lady Blackbourne would go no farther until he answered her question. The Sheridans, along with Lord and Lady Huntsleigh, not to mention the Marquess and Marchioness of Ellesmere, who had raised Marcus, were a tight group who protected each other in such a way it reminded Miles of a pack of wolves. Any threat to one member of the pack was a threat to all, and would be dealt with swiftly with less than pleasant results.

What must it be like to have such a close conclave of friends such as that? Miles could not name a single individual who would treat him in such a manner. While he had plenty of acquaintances, he had no close friends.

"I admit I very much like the idea of having a brother." The words came quietly, sneaking out from that part of him that held his secrets and his desires hostage.

Lady Blackbourne smiled and reached out to touch his sleeve. "I can attest that a brother is a most wonderful thing to have. Now, come. I have put your room two doors down from Marcus and Rebecca. I expect them to arrive with the twins tomorrow. Have you had the opportunity to meet Ellis and Lilith yet?"

The Bowens' had named their daughter after Marcus's mother, who had died shortly after his birth, and their son after his grandparents, Lord and Lady Ellesmere, who had taken Marcus in as a young boy and raised him as their ward.

"I have not."

"Well then, you are in for a treat, my lord. And I do hope you like children, as I feel you will be inundated. I should warn you, we are not in the habit of leaving them locked away in the nursery, so likely they will be underfoot more often than not."

"I'm afraid I have little experience with children, my lady, but I suppose it shall be good practice for the future, hm?"

Lady Blackbourne let out a merry laugh. "You may change your mind on that claim when you are dodging small bodies running about like wild animals."

He lifted his eyebrows at her description. Was it really like that? He had always expected to have children. He required an heir, after all. But his thoughts never went beyond that. He had assumed the actual raising of the children would be done by nannies, similar to his own upbringing. That they would be running amok amongst the adults seemed quite unorthodox.

Then again, from all he'd heard and seen from both the Sheridans and the Laythams, unorthodox was an apt description.

Was it any wonder Miss Elmsley held the couple in such high esteem?

CHAPTER FOUR

Patience pressed a nervous hand against the midnight navy silk of her ball gown, smoothing the material down. Mother had spared no expense in outfitting her for the parties and entertainments to take place over the next three weeks. Patience didn't fool herself into thinking it was for any other reason than the vain hope the appearance of quality would somehow diminish some, if not all, of her past misdeeds and catch a gentleman's attention.

"Stop fussing," Charlie said, nudging her with his elbow as they entered the large ballroom. To think this ballroom was considered the smaller of the two housed within Sheridan Park. It boggled the mind.

"How can I not," she whispered. How did anyone find their way around the vastness of the main house? Why the entry hall alone could have easily fit Havelock's sitting room into it with room to spare! "I swear, Charlie, I will get lost on my way to the refreshment room, left to wander the halls of Sheridan Park for all eternity."

Her brother chuckled. "I promise, if I notice you've been gone for too long I shall find the most handsome of the unattached gentlemen present to comb the cavernous rooms until you are found."

"Mother would love that," Patience muttered, staring at her mother's back as she and Charlie trailed a few steps behind their parents. Mother would be pleased for any situation that brought Patience to the attention of a handsome, unattached gentleman. Heavens, he would not even have to be handsome for Mother to be content. Simply unattached. And willing to change such circumstances to marry her nearly-on-the-shelf daughter. Poor Mother was growing rather desperate.

Charlie patted her hand where it rested on his forearm. "Don't look so glum, sis. I have no doubt that somewhere within this crush, you will find a gentleman to your liking. Although I must admit, I was hoping you and Walkerton might hit it off during your travels. He isn't a bad sort once you get to know him, and after two rejections I would think he'd be ripe for the picking."

"Lord Walkerton is far too stuffy for my liking, thank you." Though, even as she made her claim, the image of his smile from the other day flashed through her mind and sent a jolt of warmth flooding through her belly.

"Oh, he's a bit stern in his opinions and insistence on proper behavior, I'll give you that, but nothing someone of your sunny nature couldn't overcome, I'm certain."

Patience glanced up at her brother's smiling face. "Then you grossly overestimate my capabilities. Lord Walkerton is too resolute in his pursuits for me to be of any interest to him. He is determined to find himself a very proper, very boring lady for a wife and I cannot imagine life with a man who believes these two things are the perfect criteria for a marriage."

Charlie chuckled, as they were absorbed into the crowd like Jonah swallowed by the whale. Patience took a deep breath to quell her nerves. What did she have to be nervous about, after all? Yes, Mother had high hopes this festive season would bring the gift of a proposal for her wayward daughter, but that was nothing new. Mother had been harboring this particular wish since the day Patience was presented at court and every day following that. Her desire had come to naught, but such failure was not enough to keep Lady Beatris Elmsley from her resolve of seeing her only daughter well married. As Mother was fond of saying, Scots were not easily swayed from an intended course once they had set upon it. But as determined as Mother was to see her married, Patience was equally as determined to see herself married to the right person. To someone who would accept her for who she was and love her regardless.

She glanced around the ballroom, attempting to peer over the sea of heads in the hopes of finding a friendly face. Hen would not be here. She and her new husband, Lord Rothbury, had retired to Breckenridge for her confinement; his lordship watching over his new wife like a hawk as they anxiously awaited the arrival of their new son or daughter. Speaking of hawks, however, Lord and Lady Hawksmoor *were* expected to arrive at Sheridan Park this evening. Patience was particularly fond of the couple. Madalene, a former servant of Mr. Bowen, was a breath of fresh air, caring little for the opinions of Society. And Lord Hawksmoor, though somewhat reformed, still had the air of a delicious rake about him. Both could be counted on to be entertaining.

"There you are!"

Charlie stopped and Patience turned toward the sound of Judith's familiar voice before being scooped into her arms for a hug. She released Patience and repeated the gesture with Charlie.

"Ah, Cousin! How is my lady this fine evening?" Charlie said, his face brightening. They had not seen much of the new Lady Glenmor of late, as she and her husband, Benedict, spent much time at Maple Glen overseeing the repairs and renovations to his family's country estate.

"Much better now that I have found you," Judith said. "Heavens, I had not expected such a crush! I think every last villager in the county has made their way to Sheridan Park to take part in the festivities."

Lord and Lady Blackbourne had opened their home to lords and ladies, but also to the local gentry and those from the village wishing to make the journey to the Park and enjoy the first night of the festivities. Abigail was insistent upon carrying on her father's teachings that a title did not make you any better or any worse than the common workingman. A lesson her husband, the earl, was more than pleased to support.

"Charlie, would you mind overly much if I stole your sister for a few nights? Abby and Nicholas still have a few rooms to spare and I would so very much like to have a good catch up with Patience.

I've spoke with Aunt Beatris and she is willing to part with you for a short duration."

"You wish me to stay here? At Sheridan Park?"

"Indeed. Please say yes. I have missed you and once the festivities are over, Ben and I will be returning to Maple Glen until the beginning of the Season."

"But I have not a thing to wear save what I have on."

Judith waved a hand. "You are much the same size as Abby. She will think nothing of lending you a dress or two until Aunt Beatris can send a trunk on the morrow."

"You wish me to borrow the Countess of Blackbourne's dresses?" Mother would die. Though whether from glee or embarrassment, Patience could not rightly say.

Judith laughed. "It is Abby. She cares little of such things and she is more than happy to have you stay with us. She tells me she wishes more ladies had your kind of spirit."

It was Charlie's turn to laugh. "Is that what they're calling it these days?"

Patience elbowed her brother at the same time Judith swatted his arm.

"Very well. I will stay," Patience said. What a story it would make for later in life when she told her children about the day their mother pranced about Sheridan Park wearing a countess's gowns.

"Wonderful!" Judith gave her another hug. "Now, come. Aunt Beatris made me promise to introduce you to as many suitable gentlemen as possible as payment for allowing you to stay with me for a few days."

Patience let her head fall back and groaned, much to her brother's amusement.

Miles offered a tight smile to the young lady and her mother—their names already forgotten, lost in the miasma of all the other names heaped upon him since his arrival less than an hour previously. It seemed Lord and Lady Blackbourne had opened their ballroom to everyone within a ten-mile radius and every last one had accepted the invitation. There were lords and ladies, misters and missuses, misses and masters. So far, he'd been introduced to a blacksmith's daughter, who had eyed him as if he were a dessert and she had a sweet tooth, Marcus's steward, Mr. Cosgrove, whose daughter had married Lord Hawksmoor, and a round little barrister who spit while conversing. He'd also spoken briefly with The Hawk, himself—the man still held an air of a danger about him, causing Miles to question the claims that Lord Hawksmoor was fully reformed.

How odd to see such a mix of classes mingling in the ballroom as if such things were de rigueur. Why he had actually heard the esteemed Marchioness of Ellesmere swapping a recipe for sweet cakes with the Earl of Blackbourne's cook!

It was a strange, strange world he had entered this evening and he wasn't quite sure what to do with himself while standing in the middle of it. He had hoped to find Marcus, but so far, the man had not shown himself.

Mother had been beside herself, horrified at the blending of classes to such a point it took less than an hour for her to claim a headache and take refuge in her room. A relief, really. Miles did not have the patience to deal with her this evening.

Patience.

The name rippled through him. He had not spied her as yet; though the fact that he hoped to, if only to see a friendly face in the crowd, spoke to his level of desperation. He was out of his depth. Perhaps Mother had been right and coming here was a mistake.

"You look somewhat out of sorts, my lord."

Miles turned to his left and stared down at the face tilted upward; what could only be described as an impish smile spread across her pretty features. For a moment, he did nothing but stare, unsure whether or not he had simply conjured her image in response to his desire to see her, or if she truly stood there. Initially, he leaned toward the former, as he had never seen her appear so resplendent. Her golden hair with its shards of pale red was piled atop her head and fat, loopy curls cascaded downward to touch her bare shoulders in the most tantalizing way. The dress she wore was a shade that rested somewhere between deep blue and midnight, depending on how the light caught it and her eyes—he took a deep breath—well her eyes were nothing short of captivating, sparkling brighter than the glass beads sewn into the bodice of her gown.

But then she spoke and reality descended, informing him without pretense that the image he looked upon was, in fact, quite real.

Miss Elmsley raised one eyebrow. "Have you lost your ability to speak since I saw you last, my lord?"

His mouth tightened. "I have not. Have you sought me out to torment me with your special brand of wit this evening, Miss Elmsley?" Deuce it! That was rude, but before he could apologize, as surely he should, she shoved her hand toward him. He took it and bowed over the dainty silk glove. For a fleeting second he considered lifting those fingers to his lips and kissing them, an idea that held an unanticipated appeal.

"I came over to give you the opportunity to claim a dance before they were all spoken for. I know you would be most put out if you lost your chance to spend more time in my company while I ply you with—what did you call it?—my special brand of wit."

"Ah."

He'd never met a lady who behaved in such a forward manner before. Not only had she boldly approached him on her own, but her forthright manner of speaking left him off kilter. How did one respond to such a request? Was it even a request? It had been presented more as a statement. A fait accompli.

Admittedly, dancing with her held the same appeal as kissing her hand and he could not deny that her impish grin inspired vivid images of kissing her mouth. Blast it! None of these thoughts belonged anywhere in his head. At all. Miss Elmsley was danger personified. She was ruin waiting to happen and entertaining ideas of kissing any part of her was…well, it was…appealing—oh, damn and hell!

"*Ah*? Is that all you have to say as I stand here awaiting your answer with bated breath? I had been told you were the soul of propriety and proper manners, Lord Walkerton, but I am beginning to doubt this claim."

If she could see the images currently rampaging through his mind's eye she would understand just how accurate her doubt on this matter was.

With a resigned sigh, he nodded and acquiesced to her bold offer. "And what dances do you have left available?"

She rhymed off the names of who had claimed which dance. Many of the names he did not recognize, save for the spitting barrister.

Should he warn her about that?

The others, anyone would know. The three earls, Lords Hawksmoor, Huntsleigh and Blackbourne—all of who were already married. In fact, there was not a single, marriageable gentleman of quality anywhere on the list, save for Charlie, who was her brother and obviously did not count.

"Which leaves you the fortunate opportunity to choose the second or third waltz," she said.

"Fantastic." He forced a smile. "Then I shall choose the second waltz."

"Perfect! I do hate sitting out the waltz, my lord. It is my most favorite dance. Don't you love the way you glide across the floor like you're floating, spinning, and whirling about as if you have wings upon your feet?"

"I can claim, with all certainty, that I have never once felt as if I have had wings upon my feet," he said. Though something about the fanciful way she described the waltz made him wonder if he had been doing it wrong all these years and the sudden need to change that, assaulted him. What must it be like to feel the kind of lightness that allowed one to float and spin and glide and whirl?

Miss Elmsley tapped his chest with her folded fan. "Do you know what your problem is, my lord?"

As a matter of fact, Miles could recite a long list of his current problems. Troubles and tribulations he'd inherited from his father that dogged him from morning to night. The daily berating from his mother about his duty to resurrect the family name and restore it to its former glory. The constant stress ensuring each step he made stayed within the bounds of the strictest propriety. Unfortunately, while staring down at Patience's lovely countenance, that somehow managed to glow despite the dim lighting from a high-placed candelabrum, these troubles dissolved into the ether, leaving him unable to name even one and relying on her good will to assist in that matter.

"Pray tell, Miss Elmsley, what is my problem?"

"You suffer from a profound lack of joy."

"Joy?" A foreign concept to be sure.

"Yes. I have given the matter some thought—"

"You have?" She had thought about him?

"Yes, and I firmly believe that you should do something about it." The earnest expression on her face, as if she were truly concerned about him, took him aback almost as much as the startling accuracy of her plainspoken statement. Because she was right. He did not feel joy. Nor could he remember a moment in the near or distant past when he could claim to have done so.

"And what would you suggest I do about this lack of joy?"

"Find what makes you happy. What makes you smile. And then pursue it with a passion that makes you giddy with laughter."

He was quite certain he had never been giddy a day in his life. It sounded frightfully...wonderful. "That sounds positively foolish."

"On the contrary, it is you who would be foolish if you did not pursue such a thing with all you are worth. Life is short, my lord. If you do not embrace joy and happiness, are you not wasting your time? After all, it isn't as if you are going to be lying upon your deathbed saying, *'Goodness, I am so glad I spent my days steeped in misery and gloom.'* No one ever says that."

He scowled down at her. "I am not miserable." *Liar.* "And how would you know what people think on their deathbed?"

She shrugged. "It is common sense that a life spent in happiness is better than a life spent in bitterness."

"I am not bitter." Except he was, and no amount of denying would change that.

He was bitter that his father had been a miserable son of a bitch who forced himself upon innocent women. Bitter that a man who barely gave him more than a passing glance his entire life could reach beyond the grave to stain Miles's reputation. Bitter that Society waited with bated breath for him to make one misstep and prove he was no better. Bitter that in order to prove them wrong he must forgo pursing a life of happiness and instead live a life bound by absolute propriety.

A sacrifice he made in the hopes that one day, he may get out from under the oppressive weight of this burden. That his future children would not inherit it. That his mother would give him some peace and people would stop associating the name Radcliffe with the horrors his father had perpetrated.

Miss Elmsley said nothing in response, instead choosing to stare up at him until her sharp scrutiny made him shift his feet. Those sparkling eyes possessed the power to delve deep inside of him where he kept his secret desires buried beneath resentment and disappointment.

Could she see them? Did she know how badly he wished to set them free? To shuck off this duty to be better than his father that had been forced upon him? Did she know how badly he wished to breathe the untainted air of such freedom?

The soft smile she offered said she did and something about that frightened him. Because her smile tempted. It tempted in a way no other smile from any other lady ever had. Not Lady Rebecca. Not Lady Henrietta. No one.

Because her smile whispered, she could set him free. With one kiss. One touch. And if she did, he would be lost forever.

He took a quick step back and sucked in a deep breath as if the stifled air of the ballroom could cleanse his lungs of the sweetness she offered. He needed out. To get away. To strengthen the levees that kept such thoughts at bay before he was forced to endure their waltz. To hold her in his arms.

God help him.

"If you'll excuse me, Miss Elmsley. I should check on Mother. I shall see you for our dance."

He offered a curt bow and, despite the hint of rudeness such abruptness indicated, turned on his heel and marched swiftly toward the billiards room where the men traditionally gathered to partake in the Earl of Blackbourne's legendary brandy stash. A room where Miss Elmsley could not follow him and where he would be safe from the unrelenting pull he experienced whenever she was near.

CHAPTER FIVE

Lord Walkerton held Patience at arm's length to such a degree her shoulders and neck ached from the effort of holding the proper position while gliding about the room. Honestly, would it kill him to loosen his hold just a little so she might step closer? One would think she had the plague. She slowed her step, forcing him to glance her way instead of to the left or right or directly over her head as he had been doing thus far.

He adjusted his step with ease, as if dancing came as natural to him as breathing. "Is something amiss?"

"You mean other than the crick I am developing in my neck because you are holding me as if I carry a horrible disease you wish to avoid catching?"

His dark brow dipped and his mouth tightened, drawing her attention to his lips. When he kissed a lady, did he relax enough to make proper use of them, or did even his kisses convey the sternness so inherent in his behavior? It would be such a waste if that were so. He had the most beautiful mouth and when he smiled…well, she could not recall seeing a lord with such a lovely smile. Or a more elusive one.

Why, even Mr. Bowen, serious as he was, smiled more than Lord Walkerton—especially since he'd married Lady Rebecca.

"Forgive me," Lord Walkerton said. "It was not my intention to cause discomfort." His stiff arms loosened and the relief to her aching muscles was instant. She rolled her head from side to side as he led them around the ballroom.

"And what were your intentions, my lord?"

His gaze had wandered to somewhere over her shoulder once more, but her question brought it back to meet hers and a pool of warmth spread through her belly then dipped a little lower. The shock made her stumble and Lord Walkerton drew closer still to prevent her taking a spill.

Heavens! How embarrassing. She was a much better dancer than this. He must think her a bumbling fool who—my, but he smelled positively divine! She inhaled and let the scent of sandalwood and something else she could not pinpoint fill her senses. Goodness, but that wonderful aroma made her wish to slip out of his distant hold and wrap her arms around him so she might surround herself with it. A giggle escaped her, drawing a strict look from Lord Walkerton.

"Miss Elmsley, have you been imbibing this evening?"

That he asked this question with all seriousness made her laugh in earnest now, though why, she couldn't rightly say. Something about the absurdity of this moment, this interaction between them, had set loose the need to do so. The fact that she experienced this feeling in the company of one of the most humorless men of her acquaintance only made keeping a straight face all the more impossible.

Which appeared to annoy his lordship to no end, making her laugh all the more.

"Miss Elmsley, please get a hold of yourself. You are drawing attention."

She bit her lip and regained a modicum of control long enough to utter, "Oh dear, how awful." But his uncompromising expression caused another burst of amusement, negating her claim completely.

A huff of exasperation brushed against her face and a tingle of sensation spread beneath her skin. "Miss Elmsley, if you do not cease this behavior at once, I will be forced to—"

"To what? Walk away? Leave me stranded on the dance floor? That won't cause any talk at all, I'm sure."

There was that tightening of the mouth again. His poor lips. They must hurt from being held in such a manner for so much of the day. Likely, they could use a proper kiss to make them feel better. The image of doing so and the look of shock that would likely erupt over Lord Walkerton's handsome features caused her shoulders to shake from the effort of holding in her laughter until tears formed in her eyes.

None of which pleased Lord Stuffy Shirt at all. His brow dipped downward and his gaze hardened until not even diamonds would cut through it. She needed to stop, but the more she tried, the more the laughter insisted on being let loose.

"Bloody hell."

Her eyebrows rose. Had Lord Stuffy Shirt just swore in front of her, a lady? Goodness, the situation must be dire!

He brought her closer still. Oh, this was nice. Much easier on the arms and neck and my, but that heavenly scent was positively intoxicating. What would he think if she told him the only thing she had imbibed upon was the delectable masculine aroma surrounding him? Likely, that would be the thing that sent him running from the ballroom, never to be seen again.

"Please, Miss Elmsley. Get control of yourself."

She glanced up, his face only inches from hers now that he had pulled her in as if to smother the sound of her laughter. He had recently shaved; his smooth skin held the scent of bay rum and there was the smallest nick along the edge of his jaw. Something about that imperfection spoke to her in a language that quieted the laughter but left her with a smile playing about the corners of her mouth.

"My lord," she said. "Why do you insist on pushing away joy as if even the smallest bit might set about a catastrophic event? What is it you're so afraid of?"

"Nothing." Miles ground out the lie between clenched teeth. Would this infernal waltz never end?

Her question set Miles on edge. Damnation, everything about Miss Elmsley set him on edge. She possessed a captivating charm that tempted him down a merry path he sorely wished to travel, but could not. He knew this. Understood it with a firmness that brooked no wavering. Following her would lead to ruin. Allowing her to break through his barriers and persuade him to behave without thought to consequences would undo all the reparations to his family name he had accomplished thus far. Should he let go, should he step even a little outside the bounds of propriety, Society would turn on him with swift retribution. They would take this lapse as proof he was heading down the same path as his father, choosing scandal over proper behavior, thinking with the wrong part of his anatomy. They would shake their collective heads in disdain and whisper, *'Ah, yes. Just like his father, that one. Well, it was to be expected. The apple never falls far from the tree, does it?'*

Perhaps he should have risked rudeness and refused to accept Miss Elmsley's demand he claim a dance, dangling the offer in front of him like a mesmerist's watch. He should have known better.

A dance was a very dangerous thing. A waltz even more so. Especially a waltz with the frustratingly tantalizing Miss Patience Elmsley. That was nothing short of a catastrophe waiting to happen.

What had he been thinking?

His mouth tightened and he drew in a deep breath. He had not been thinking. At least not with his brain. Instead, his body had taken over. The enticing memory of how it felt to hold her against him when the broken carriage wheel catapulted her into his arms, and the desire to do so again, had trampled his good sense into submission. Her ready smile sparked a desire in him that had kindled during the hours spent sitting only a few feet away from her. Her energy enveloped him, drew him in, made promises he desperately wanted to believe in.

She faced life as if it was a mystery she was eager to explore and Miles could not deny something about her openness made him equally eager to explore her. A fact that had kept him from experiencing a decent night's sleep since leaving The Burly Oak Inn. Each time he closed his eyes the dangerous vision of her in his arms, the unexpected rightness of her against him, tormented his mind. Not to mention other areas in his body farther south.

Miles made a slight misstep, enough to lift one of Miss Elmsley's golden eyebrows in question. A question Miles had no intention of answering. God forbid. He did not even want to think what disaster would come about should he voice the thoughts clamoring about his head. Would she be shocked? Or would she be amenable to them? No! It did not matter. Such thoughts were to be shoved down into the deep, dark recesses of his mind and left there.

"Forgive me," he said, though whether he apologized for the misstep or the scandalous images of her in his head, he could not quite determine.

She sighed and her sweet breath brushed against his skin like a caress. For the briefest second, he closed his eyes. Welcomed the sensation. Longed for more.

"I am a constant irritation to you, aren't I, my lord."

Miles opened his eyes and stared at Miss Elmsley's open expression. "Yes, I suppose you are."

The answer was out of him before he could call the words back to rephrase them properly, to explain that the irritation had little to do with her, per se, and everything to do with the unwanted feelings she evoked within him. But he could not tell her this despite the hurt that now darkened her lovely blue eyes and made him wish differently.

He had not come here to dally with the likes of Miss Elmsley. He had come to Sheridan Park this Christmas to strengthen his relationship with Marcus Bowen and find a sense of connection to family he had gone his entire life without, and, if luck prevailed, to find a proper bride.

Neither of these undertakings involved Miss Elmsley in any way.

And yet, at every turn, there she was. He could not take a step without tripping over her, thinking about her, being tormented by the very ideas she pushed upon him.

"Then I shall try to avoid you as much as possible for the duration of the festivities," she said, lifting her chin high, though not so high he missed how deeply his words had sliced into her natural happiness, cutting through its fabric and letting a little of the joy bleed out.

Bloody hell.

"Miss Elmsley, forgive—"

She stopped moving as the music ended and yanked her hand from his, taking a step back.

"Good evening, my lord." She offered a sharp curtsey and spun on her heel, marching away from him with solid purpose.

Only to run smack into the squat Mr. Butterfield. The portly gentleman grabbed hold of her as he staggered backward directly into old Lady Mertle, who back-peddled into a potted plant, toppling it over as she fell, gripping the tails of Mr.

Butterfield's jacket. And before anyone could stop them, all three fell to the floor in a heap of tangled limbs with Miss Elmsley on top, her skirts hiked up well past her knee to show off a very pretty embroidered garter, a lovely ankle and a very shapely calf for all to see.

CHAPTER SIX

"If it is any consolation at all, there were plenty of attendees who missed witnessing the incident entirely," Judith said, coming over to the bed and sitting next to Patience.

"She is right," Charlie said from his spot on the opposite side of her, giving her a one-armed hug. "Most had to console themselves with only hearing about it second or third hand."

Judith reached across Patience and swatted her cousin as Patience groaned and buried her face in her hands. "Mother must be beside herself." The words were muffled against her silk gloves, but the pat on her back from Charlie was enough of an acknowledgement to indicate the truth in her assumption.

"I'm certain Aunt Beatris will be fine. It wasn't your fault, after all. Mr. Butterfield all but grabbed you and hauled you down upon him."

"Lord, that sounds rather salacious when you say it that way, Jude. Maybe choose a different set of words when speaking with Mother," Charlie suggested.

Patience looked up. The burn of humiliation still scalded her skin. The entire debacle had happened so fast it passed through her mind in a flash. She had spun away from Lord Walkerton, wishing to do nothing more than to escape his hurtful words. She hadn't even seen Mr. Butterfield in her path—which seemed a little hard to imagine given his short, squat stature would have put him squarely at eye level. But she had been up in her head, as Mother liked to call it, reliving the moment Lord Walkerton had freely admitted he felt nothing more toward her than a solid case of irritation.

Why such a claim had hurt so deeply, she was determined not to explore, but regardless the reason, it had blinded her to Mr. Butterfield's presence. Could hurt temporarily blind someone? Apparently so, given she'd run smack into the poor man, sending them both spinning and falling until she had landed on top of the heap of bodies—fully exposing herself from ankle to thigh for all to see.

Her only consolation was that she had worn her loveliest stockings with the bluebells embroidered up the back of the calf. That was something, at least.

Not that Lord Walkerton had appeared to care much about her stockings if the shock written across his handsome features was any indication. She'd never seen a man appear so scandalized before. Why, he had practically been frozen in place for the first few seconds before he reacted and offered her a hand up.

He'd barely said a word to her, other than to inquire if she was hurt—which she was not, unless one was referring to her pride. That had suffered a rather grievous, potentially fatal injury. So much for a smooth getaway. Instead of stomping off with her nose in the air, she had caused an embarrassing debacle and lived up to every preconceived notion he had of her.

Had he bothered to meet her gaze when lending her a hand up, likely she would have seen disappointment and resignation darkening those lovely hazel eyes. But he hadn't met her gaze. He'd released her hand the moment she found her feet as if she were a hot, burning coal. Others had already helped Mr. Butterfield and Lady Mertle up, the former loudly expressing his horror at having landing squarely upon Lady Mertle, though from the hungry gleam in the older lady's eyes, it appeared the grand lady was the only one out of the trio that hadn't minded what had happened.

Then again, Lady Mertle's skirts had stayed firmly about her ankles, pinned there by Mr. Butterfield's ample weight, while Patience's skirts had hiked upward, flashing everyone who had a clear view of the incident.

Heat flamed up her face once more.

"Mother will never let me hear the end of this. I had hoped to at least hold off causing any kind of embarrassment to our parents until the final days of the festivities."

Charlie smiled and drew her close to his side. "There, there, pet. I'm certain by now Mother and Father are used to such spectacles from you and any irritation they're experiencing will be over by morning."

His words did little to ease her concern, especially one word in particular. *Irritation*. Was that how everyone—not just Lord Walkerton—saw her? As an irritation? It wasn't as if she went out of her way to make a spectacle of herself. It was just that sometimes she said or did things in the moment because instinct told her it was the right thing to say or do. Such as dumping the bowl of punch over Lady Susan's head when she insulted Judith. Then other times, such as tonight, things just *happened.* It wasn't as if she had intentionally blundered into Mr. Butterfield. She was only trying to get away from Lord Walkerton's belief that she was…well, that she was exactly what she'd just proved herself to be.

An irritation. An embarrassment.

Was it any wonder Mother and Father wanted so badly to have her married off? That way she would cease to be their problem.

The sad realization settled upon her heart, pressing heavily into it until it ached. What a burden she must be to her family. How they must always feel as if they were dangling from tenterhooks, waiting for her to do something to embarrass herself and by extension, her family. How badly they must want rid of such a burden. Maybe she should loosen her grasp on the idea of marrying for love and let Mother and Father choose a suitable husband, if for no other reason than to give them some respite from her inability to stop embarrassing herself. And them.

"I think I should like to stay in my room for the rest of the evening," Patience said. Going back downstairs to join the party was too much to bear. Better she stay up here where she could not cause any further damage.

"Would you like me to stay with you?" Judith asked, but Patience shook her head. She would not be good company and there was no point in having her cousin miss spending time with her new family because of Patience's latest farce.

No, best she sequester herself for this evening. She had some decisions to make about her future.

Miles tossed the heavy blankets aside, sat up, and swung his legs over the edge of the bed. The polished wood was cold beneath his feet, the fire from the hearth having burned down through the night until only embers remained. The cool air nipped at his bare skin and he reached for his dressing gown. He pulled it on and crossed the bedchamber to stoke the fire, waking it from its slumber.

Once the flames reappeared, he let it be and moved to the window, rubbing his arms to spark some warmth. He pulled back the heavy curtain and looked up at the cloudless sky. A deep breath slowly escaped him. Given the position of the moon, it could be no more than half past three in the morning. He'd been awake for hours, having left the party early.

Really, after one had witnessed the glorious display of Miss Elmsley's shapely calf and delicate stockings, what else could the party possibly have to offer? Unfortunately, he could not wrestle the image from his mind nor douse the hot flash of desire that had shot through him upon witnessing it.

For a brief moment, he'd been unable to move. While his good sense insisted he help her up, the rest of him was frozen in place, wishing not to disturb the lovely visual feast set out before him.

Thankfully, his sense of decency overcame his baser instincts and he'd pulled her to her feet before the majority of the crowd could witness such. The horror imprinted on her exquisite features, the swiftness with which she retracted her hand from his, cut him to the core. But heavens, the aplomb she showed in the aftermath, well, that was a thing of beauty.

Head held high, she turned on her heel and faced Mr. Butterfield and Lady Mertle, begged their forgiveness for her clumsiness, inquired upon any injury they may have incurred, then, upon learning all was well, set her shoulders back and walked from the ballroom with the unhurried pace of a lady who had nowhere of import to be.

It had all been a lie, of course. Because he had followed her from the room and saw that once she thought herself alone, had picked her skirts up and ran up the stairs as if someone had set fire to her slippers. And his heart broke a little for her in that moment. He didn't want it to. He did not want his heart anywhere in the near vicinity of her. If anything, the debacle he'd just witnessed was vintage Miss Elmsley behavior. It verified every misgiving he held about her—that she could not get through an event without causing some sort of scene or disturbance.

And yet…

And yet.

Miles gritted his teeth against the truth, but that did not stop it from coming. And the truth was he could not erase her image from his mind. He could not ignore the pain that had flashed through her eyes when he'd helped her up. Not physical pain, but something that went far deeper. And that pain had reached out to him. Called to him in a quiet way that made him want to fix the hurt. Or worse, to protect her from it.

Such foolishness! He released the curtain and let it fall back into place, shrouding the room in darkness, save for the weak light from the lamp he'd left burning next to his bed. Wrapping his dressing gown more tightly around him, he left his bedchamber. Perhaps a change of scenery would alleviate the strange and unwelcomed feelings Miss Patience Elmsley aroused within him.

Miles quietly roamed the labyrinth of hallways, keeping to the shadows as much as he could, but the walk about the great manor did little to alleviate the mixed emotions that haunted him. He saw no one during his travels. No lord or lady slipping from their assigned bedchamber to visit another, not even a maid of all work scurrying under the cover of darkness to do whatever tasks she had yet to complete. He was completely alone.

A state he should be used to, yet one that had begun to chafe as one by one, his acquaintances paired off with newly acquired spouses and the two ladies he thought to do the same with instead fell in love with other gentlemen, leaving him high and dry. And the uncomfortable thought, the one he had tried to avoid for most of his life, had grown steadily louder.

Would he always be alone? Was his father's atrocious behavior enough of a deterrent to keep any respectable lady from setting her cap for him?

For the longest time, he'd ignored that particular thought. Told himself that it did not matter as he'd always been a bit of a solitary soul, whether through choice or consequence. But lately something had changed. Lately he'd come to realize that he was, well, lonely.

Miles stopped walking as he reached the atria and the truth of his situation sank in. Finally admitting to his loneliness however offered no comfort. And though he planned—hoped—to marry a woman of impeccable reputation and settle into married life sooner, rather than later, he could not confidently say that he expected marriage to alter his state of loneliness. After all, his new wife would be little more than a stranger to him. Perhaps over time, that would change, but what if it didn't? It certainly hadn't for his parents. Their inherent dislike of each other had cast a pall over his entire life. Would he suffer the same fate?

"What of love and laughter and silliness and fun? Do you not wish for any of those things?"

Miss Elmsley's pointed question came back to haunt him, pressing against his secret fears and making them grow. He did not recall ever experiencing those things, so to imagine he wished for them was beyond his capabilities. And so he grasped at what he did know. Propriety. Avoidance of all things scandalous. Anything and everything that would distance him from his father's despicable acts. Perhaps if he could achieve this, contentment would come. It wasn't the same as happiness, not to hear Miss Elmsley describe it, but it was the best he could hope for, given the circumstances.

Miles walked over to one of the benches placed between the large windows that lined the atria and sat facing generations of past Earls of Blackbourne. All were stern of face, their grim visages glaring out at all who passed by. Only the current earl's painting held a spark of life within his dark features, the way the edge of his mouth quirked upward on one side and the corners of his eyes crinkled in amusement. As if he knew a secret.

Perhaps the secret was the type of marriage Miss Elmsley had alluded to. Miles had seen Lord and Lady Blackbourne together on any number of occasions and their love for each other was a clear and palpable thing. Their frequent public displays of affection bordered on the scandalous, though neither of them showed the least bit of contrition over such. Lord and Lady Huntsleigh were no better, come to think of it. Even his half brother, though far more self-contained than either Lords Blackbourne or Huntsleigh, was clearly in love with his wife and could barely remove his gaze from her whenever they were in the same room.

And do not even get him started on Lord Hawksmoor and his new bride, though perhaps that type of behavior was to be expected from one as notorious as The Hawk, who went so far as to marry a servant, of all things. Though one would never guess the current Lady Hawksmoor was anything but a lady if they did not know their story and after meeting her, he had to admit the young lady had mightily impressed him.

Miles let out a slow sigh that sounded rather pathetic even to his ears and he was glad he was the only one to hear it. The simple fact was he led a solitary life of duty and monotony. All attempts thus far at finding a proper bride had been met with abject failure despite his title and adequate fortune. And so he remained as he had always been.

Alone.

The truth of this slipped in around him like a dark shadow. It was a sad commentary to realize he had no true close friends. Acquaintances, yes, but he had never allowed himself to cultivate anything beyond that. A part of him did not feel worthy. That the things his father had done made him somehow less. A belief echoed by the fact even his relatives kept their distance, unwilling to build any close ties, as if the scandal was something communicable.

Miles could count on one hand those who appeared to care little about the stain of his father's actions. Charlie Elmsley, for one. Given his sister's antics, likely a bit of scandal was not something to deter him. And Miles's newly discovered half brother, Marcus Bowen. Thoughtful and intelligent, the man was fair in his judgments despite having the best reason of all for despising the Radcliffe name.

And, of course, Miss Patience Elmsley, who, Miles had discovered, shied away from very little, but rather flung herself with great gusto into every moment life had to offer. Miss Elmsley, for all her faults, had the uncanny ability to look forward, to leave the past behind as if it traveled far too slowly to keep up with her. Likely, a much-needed skill on her part, all things considered.

"Have you lost your way within the catacombs of Nick's humble abode?"

Miles glanced up, startled by the voice that had crept up on him without notice, and found Marcus staring down at him, holding two bundles in his arms. He too, was wearing a dressing gown, and the moonlight that spilled through the window showed his hair was pushed about, this way and that, as if he'd been awoken from a sound slumber quite rudely.

"Mr. Bowen—"

"Marcus. For heaven's sakes man, let us dispense with the formalities. And here—" Miles had no time to react before Marcus bent and shoved one squirming bundle into his arms. "Allow me to introduce you to your niece, Lily."

Lily. Named after Marcus's mother, Lilith. The young woman Miles's father had—

Miles closed his eyes and shut out the ugly thought that had no business being near an innocent child. When he reopened them, he found himself peering down into the face of an angel with round eyes and cherubic cheeks illuminated by moonlight. Lily stared up at him with great intent. One hand had worked its way free of the swaddling and reached toward him, fingers closing and opening. He held out his own finger and she gripped onto it with a strength that surprised him, drawing it to her mouth where she proceeded to gum at it, covering it in drool. And then she smiled and it was as if sunlight had invaded the room and chased away the shadows.

"Watch out for her," Marcus warned, taking the seat next to him on the bench and leaning his back against the wall. "She has inherited her mother's charm."

"Ah." Miles smiled. He was well acquainted with Lady Rebecca's charm. It was what had originally drawn him to her. She had always had a way about her, one part warmth and one part wit. Perhaps had he capitalized on her infatuation with him when it had occurred, instead of waffling due to her brother's scandalous reputation as he had, it would be their babe he held in his arms. But in the end, he *had* waffled and the man who loved her with far more depth than Miles ever had, had won her over with such completeness there could be no question that things had turned out the way they should. "She's quite lovely."

"You may rethink that when you hear her caterwauling in the wee hours of the morning, waking her brother who then decides to join her in an act of sibling solidarity."

Given the tired tone of Marcus's voice, Miles surmised this happened on a rather regular basis. It struck him as odd that Marcus would know this. Or that he would be wandering the halls with both babes in arms.

"Would the nanny not take care of the children?"

Marcus smiled down at his son, who was wide awake and quiet as a mouse, and his face filled with such love, Miles did not think he had ever witnessed such a pure and wondrous thing. Surely, his own mother had never looked upon him in such a way.

"Sometimes, but most nights Rebecca and I prefer to have them close. I was not raised by nannies and so the idea is a bit foreign to me. In the middle of the night when I awoke from bad dreams, it was my mother who comforted me and it is those memories of her I hold most dear. I wish for my children to experience that same kind of love from their parents that I did, to have memories of us offering them comfort when they needed it, not a hired stranger."

The reverence, with which Marcus spoke of the couple that had given him their name and raised him until their untimely passing, surprised Miles. The Bowens had not been his blood, yet they had offered Marcus more love and support in the short time he had been with them than Miles's own parents had given him throughout his life. And now Marcus and Lady Rebecca would pass the same onto their children, and they would grow into adults knowing they were valued and loved beyond all measure. What a gift to bestow upon a child.

"And so I have taken to walking the halls in an effort to quiet the little tyrants so my lovely wife might sleep," Marcus said then turned his gaze in Miles's direction. "And what brings you here?"

Miles opened his mouth then promptly closed it. What was he to say? That he could not stop thinking about Miss Elmsley's perfectly shaped calf or the look that had darkened her blue eyes when he'd readily agreed with her assessment that he found her a constant irritation? Oh, if he could take those words back he would in a heartbeat. But it was too late. She had turned away from him and in doing so, set off a calamitous event that left her humiliated.

"I believe I said something I should not have and it is too late to undo the damage my words caused." The admission slipped out into the darkness, surprising him. He was not one to confide in others.

"Ah. Woman troubles then."

"I did not say that."

Marcus laughed quietly and his son gurgled in response. "You didn't have to. You're wandering about in the dark in the wee hours of the morning, fretting over something you said. Only a woman could send a man to such depths of despair he gives up a good night's sleep over it. Should I assume the woman in question is Miss Elmsley?"

"I don't know what would give you that impression."

Another quiet laugh. "I'll take that as a yes then. What did you say?"

Marcus Bowen's astute powers of observation were well known among the ton, so it should come as no surprise to Miles that he had taken notice of whatever it was that had cropped up between him and Miss Elmsley. But it did surprise. Miles was not accustomed to having anyone pay such close attention—as if his actions were worthy of their notice.

"It is of little importance."

"If it were of such little import, you would not be sitting here in the dark, worrying over it."

Miles pulled his mouth into a grim line. He was unaccustomed to having someone with whom to discuss his problems. Then again, Marcus *was* his brother, though newly discovered, and wasn't such a discussion best had between brothers? He wasn't sure, but it wasn't as if he had anyone else to talk to and he'd certainly not come up with any viable solution on his own.

"Miss Elmsley asked me, as we were waltzing, if I viewed her as nothing more than a constant source of irritation."

"And you said?"

Miles closed his eyes and let out a hard breath. "I may have said yes." He opened his eyes in time to see Marcus wince.

"Bloody hell, Miles. What were you thinking?"

"I was thinking that she *was* a constant irritation, just not—" He stopped, the words he was about to say lingering on the tip of his tongue. *Just not in the way she meant.* He swallowed them whole, hoping they would return to the dark netherworld they'd crept out of and stay there. "Regardless, it hurt her feelings and in an effort to hastily depart my company, she ran into Mr. Butterfield and set off a series of events that resulted in her humiliation."

Marcus's lips twitched but he held back his smile, though one dark eyebrow arched skyward. "Well, I can see only one course of action you can take to remedy the situation you've caused."

A sliver of relief filled Miles at Marcus's indication he had a solution to the problem. "What must I do?"

"Marry her."

CHAPTER SEVEN

"I beg your pardon?" Obviously, his brother was mad. Completely and irreversibly insane. He'd never heard a more preposterous suggestion. "Marry her?"

Lily squirmed in his arms and Miles jostled her slightly until she resettled. How oddly comforting the weight of this tiny human felt in his arms. He glanced down at her. Would she one day send a man into such fits? She smiled and blinked at him. Likely.

"Yes, marry her," Marcus repeated, but it sounded no less crazy the second time he said it.

"I am not interested in Miss Elmslcy."

"And yet here you sit in the dark in the middle of the night, worrying over having injured her tender feelings." His brother smiled and the gesture transformed his face, lightening it in a way his normally serious expression never could.

"It is the gentlemanly thing to do after behaving in a rather ungentlemanly manner."

Marcus made a grunting sound and motioned for Miles to hand over the warm bundle in his arms. He did so, with a hint of reluctance he hadn't been prepared for. Perhaps, when he had children of his own, he would take a page from Marcus's book and use a more hands-on approach.

His brother stood and looked down at him. "A piece of advice, Miles—if you have an opportunity to find a woman with the ability to keep you up at night, you should marry her with all due haste. At least that way, when she continues to keep you up at night, it will be for a far more pleasing reason."

The image of Miss Elmsley beneath him, golden curls splayed against the white sheet of his bed and her warm, bare skin pressing into his own shot through Miles with swift purpose, startling him with its clarity.

Marcus offered a half-smile and quiet chuckle as if he was privy to the machinations of Miles's tired mind. "Good night, brother."

Except that it wasn't a good night at all and any hope he'd had of finding solace in sleep was now replaced by the unwanted idea Marcus had planted in his brain.

The last thing a man searching for a bride of unimpeachable reputation should do is marry the likes of Miss Patience Elmsley.

"Are you well acquainted with Lord and Lady Blackbourne?" Lady Charlotte Overton, daughter of the late Marquess of Willanthorpe, asked. Miles had been paired with the young lady to escort her to the awaiting sleigh with its two large draft horses decked out with bells and the occasional red bow tied to their harnesses.

"No, not particularly," Miles answered, her question interrupting his visual sweep of those already seated on the sleigh. "A passing acquaintance, at best. But Mr. Bowen and I—"

He stopped. The relationship between he and Marcus was not something he could freely speak of, for the sake of all concerned. Which meant, as much as Miles relished the new idea of having a brother, he could not claim him as such in a public way. Just as well. Imagine the scandal that would cause! Good heaven, he'd never find himself a proper bride if he openly chummed about with his bastard brother as if such things were acceptable.

Still, the idea rankled. It was decidedly unfair, in his opinion, that anyone would look down their nose at Marcus should they learn the truth, as if something he had no part in would suddenly change the fact that he was a good and honorable man.

But that was the way things were, as he knew all too well.

"Lord Walkerton?"

"Hm?" Lady Charlotte's slight pressure on his arm pulled him away from his musings. He glanced down at her. She was a pretty sort, with dark hair that reminded him of coffee before he added the cream. Her eyes were darker still and framed with thick lashes. Despite her outwardly upbeat nature, Miles sensed a lingering sadness behind her smile, as if keeping it in place took some effort.

"You didn't finish your sentence, my lord. You and Mr. Bowen are familiar then?"

"Yes," he answered and their conversation of two nights previous came back to him. He had never spoken to someone in such an open way before. Nor been able to be honest without worrying his words would be held against him. It had been a revelation. Though Marcus's own revelation that Miles should marry Miss Elmsley was so far off the mark he had to question whether the lack of sleep from squalling babies had left the man slightly addled.

Lady Charlotte inquired no further on the topic and Miles was thankful. "And are you enjoying yourself thus far, my lord?"

"Uh, yes, I suppose so," he said, as they drew closer to the sleigh. It was the easiest answer to give. The truth was far too convoluted to delve into and likely Lady Charlotte was not interested in a long dissertation on his actual feelings about another woman.

Why was it that the ladies of his acquaintance seemed overly concerned with his ability to enjoy himself? He had not come to Sheridan Park for enjoyment. He'd come to build a relationship with his brother and to hopefully find himself a bride whose past was free of scandal or impropriety. A lady such as the one he had on his arm.

Lady Charlotte had recently come out of mourning following the death of her father, an event that had caused her to miss her third Season. With her upcoming fourth Season on the horizon, and whispers of her having one foot on the shelf, she should be amenable to any overtures he made toward an association between them. He should strike while the iron was hot.

Yet Miles could not walk from the main house to the stables without his mind wandering away from the lady on his arm to rest on other things.

Or, more particularly, other people.

More precisely, one person in particular.

A person his hungry gaze searched for as they neared the awaiting sleigh. He found her easily enough, already seated and happily conversing with the man sitting next to her. A man Miles did not recognize, but immediately disliked for no other reason than his overt friendliness toward Miss Elmsley.

"Are you familiar with the gentleman sitting next to Miss Elmsley?" Miles asked Lady Charlotte, attempting as much nonchalance as he could muster. "I don't recall seeing him before today."

Lady Charlotte glanced in the general direction Miles had indicated as they reached the short line of people being assisted into the sleigh. "That is Mr. Anton Farthing. I met him when he arrived yesterday with Sir Arran. Miss Elmsley indicated he is the son of an old regimental friend of her uncle's who thought to stop at Havelock Manor on his way through the area. Lady Elmsley invited him to stay as the man had no plans for the holidays."

"I see. So he is staying at Havelock Manor then?" Which was where Miss Elmsley would be returning to tomorrow. And my, but how chummy the two appeared.

"Yes." She lowered her voice and leaned in closer so he might hear her. "It is speculated that Lady Elmsley plans to curate an affection between Mr. Farthing and her daughter, perhaps to alleviate the nonsense kicked up from the incident of the other evening."

Lady Charlotte's claims kicked Miles in the gut. "That seems a rather drastic action."

"I agree and her uncle, Sir Arran, is most opposed to the idea of the match and of keeping Mr. Farthing in such close proximity to Miss Elmsley, but apparently his wife and Lady Elmsley have overruled him in that respect. They insist that tossing Mr. Farthing out to spend the holidays alone would be most uncharitable."

"I find myself in agreement with Sir Arran on that account." Should he speak to the man about it? Push him to assert his opinion and send Mr. Farthing packing? But what right did he have to do so? It was no business of his.

"I would think any man would have to have taken complete leave of his senses to behave in an inappropriate manner with Sir Arran, not to mention Lord and Mr. Elmsley, holding you accountable for your actions. How lovely it must be to have such champions watching over you."

Miles could not argue Lady Charlotte's claim that Miss Elmsley would be safe, but that didn't mean he liked the idea of her living under the same roof as this man—this stranger—even a little bit. But in the end, his opinion on the matter held no weight. He had no claim over Miss Elmsley.

"Ah, Lady Charlotte! How splendid to see you again. You must sit next to us."

Miles did his best not to scowl at Mr. Farthing's upbeat greeting or the suggestion they sit next to him and Miss Elmsley. He had no business disliking the man on sight, but he could not help himself. Though he preferred to skip past the reasons for such a reaction. Some things were best left unacknowledged.

"Allow me." Mr. Farthing stood and offered a hand to Lady Charlotte despite the fact Miles had escorted her and was fully capable of seeing her seated.

"I have it well in hand, sir," Miles said, his tone more curt than was warranted. He took a breath. "But I thank you."

"Very well then." If the man was put off, he did not show it as he retook his seat. "Let us make room for the couple, shall we, Miss Elmsley?"

Miles hazarded a glance at Miss Elmsley, who appeared less than pleased at the new seating arrangement that put him next to her with Lady Charlotte on his other side. It was rather disorienting, having the woman who occupied far too many of his thoughts on his right and the woman more suited to his goals on his left. But the sleigh jolted as the driver snapped the reins and then they were underway, any hope of changing his seat gone.

Miss Elmsley sighed and a cloud of white puffed out of her mouth into the cold air. "I suppose I should do the introductions. Mr. Farthing, may I present to you his lordship, Miles Radcliffe, Earl of Walkerton."

It was the first time Miles had heard his full name spoken by Miss Elmsley and, much to his dismay, he loved the way it sounded. Though she appeared to derive little enjoyment in speaking it.

"And, of course, Lady Charlotte Overton. I believe you met her uncle, the Marquess of Willanthorpe, when you arrived last night, Mr. Farthing."

"Yes, of course," Her companion said in an effusive tone that grated on Miles's last nerve. "Capital man, Lady Charlotte. I found him quite entertaining."

Miles raised an eyebrow. He had met Lord Willanthorpe and found him anything but entertaining. In actuality, his impression of the marquess was that of an ill-natured gentleman who possessed all the warmth of a badger having a bad day. He pitied Lady Charlotte in living with the man and if there was any silver lining should he make an offer for her, it was that he might rescue her from the fate of being unmarried and dependent on her uncle's benevolence.

"That is kind of you to say, Mr. Farthing. I will be certain to pass along the compliment."

"And you, Lord Walkerton," Mr. Farthing said, turning his attention to Miles. "When Miss Elmsley mentioned your name, I had thought we'd once met, but the Lord Walkerton I recall was much older, more of an age with Sir Arran. It was in Italy several years ago while I was abroad."

Miles gritted his teeth until his jaw ached. "That would have been my father you met. He has since passed on."

"I see. Forgive me. And my sincerest condolences. Though I am certain the late earl's memory will live on in the hearts and minds of all, wouldn't you say?"

Miles stared at the man. Something in his expression, in the way one eyebrow lifted a fraction higher than the other, the curve of his smile, read false. Had Mr. Farthing known his father well?

Been aware of his tendencies? Was there some hint of malice beneath his words, a warning of sort?

Miles shook his head. No, of course not. Likely they had been introduced and nothing more. It wasn't as if the two would have traveled in the same social circle, after all. Still—

"Will you be attending the ball this evening, Miss Elmsley?" Lady Charlotte interrupted Miles's thoughts, as if she could sense the thin strand of disquiet the mention of his father had created.

Unfortunately, her question broached another rather sensitive topic.

"Oh," Miss Elmsley glanced down at her leather gloves and flexed her fingers, her bright smile faltering in a way that cut into Miles with acute accuracy. "I am not sure."

"Why ever not?" Mr. Farthing asked. Did the man always speak so loudly? It drew the attention of everyone within earshot. Then again, perhaps that was his intention. Regardless, it was a rather annoying trait. "I would hate to miss a chance to dance with someone as lively as yourself."

Miss Elmsley's smile recovered somewhat, though not fully. It dipped once again as she offered her explanation. "It is just that...well...I had a bit of a, uh, spill at the last ball and I'm afraid I made something of a spectacle of myself. I have been told that my penchant for drawing attention to myself in such a manner is a constant source of irritation to others."

Miles's heart twisted in his chest and guilt battered against his conscience.

"Oh, I'm certain that isn't true," Lady Charlotte said.

"On the contrary." Miss Elmsley's gaze flitted quickly in Miles's direction before returning to her hands. "I have it on good authority this is true."

The downturn in her smile, the darkening of her sunny disposition, these changes rested at his feet. He had said the hurtful words and regretted each one fervently. And while it would be most beneficial if she did not continuously make a spectacle of herself—

He straightened in his seat. Most beneficial...for him? Why? So that he might court her?

The sleigh went over a hump of packed snow and jostled its passengers. Miss Elmsley bumped against him, reaching out her hand for purchase. Her touch upon his leg was there and gone as quickly as it came, yet it seared through the wool blanket across his lap and his breeches as if no barriers existed between her hand and his flesh, arresting his thoughts. Amplifying them. Bringing to the surface Marcus's advice despite Miles's attempts to burn such from his memory.

Marry her.

No. No, no, no, no. Absolutely not. His best course of action was to concentrate on Lady Charlotte. A perfectly lovely young woman with a pleasant demeanor, unblemished reputation, and good family connections.

Yes, but, the incessant voice in his head interjected, the words buzzing about inside his mind like a bug that refused to leave no matter how many times you swatted it away.

Miles let out a sigh. But what?

She does not sparkle.

Sparkle? Well, that was the most ridiculous thing he had ever heard. As if that was some type of desirable attribute. Perhaps Lady Charlotte did not sparkle in the same manner as Miss Elmsley, but neither did she walk about with scandal nipping at her heels like a playful puppy demanding attention. Not that Miss Elmsley actively sought such scandal or even spectacle. Oftentimes, her behavior was in defense of others. Or brought on by her curious and inquisitive nature. Neither of which were horrible qualities in an individual. In fact, he found the way she stood up for others quite admirable. Unfortunately, such behavior often resulted in some type of calamity or social disaster.

And Miles had experienced enough disasters in his life to know better than to court one more, let alone marry one. No matter how much she sparkled. Or how quickly her smile traveled through him like a soothing balm. Or the way her laughter sounded like wind chimes blowing gently upon the breeze. Or how much he missed both of those things when they dimmed because of something he had said.

Bloody hell.

"You should not allow the incident from the other night to keep you from the festivities," he said to her, after silence had lapsed between the foursome.

Miss Elmsley looked up at him; her bright blue eyes round with surprise. "I beg your pardon?"

"You should not hide yourself away," he said. "What happened was an accident. No one thinks worse of you for it. Why, just this morning I saw Mr. Butterfield and Lady Mertle sitting together in the breakfast room, their heads bowed close and appearing quite taken with each other. Perhaps, had you not bumped into Mr. Butterfield, he and Lady Mertle might never have struck up a friendship."

Bullocks, he sounded like an idiot. But all thoughts of such blew away on the power of Miss Elmsley's smile.

"Do you think so?"

"I am quite certain." That he was a complete idiot and this ridiculous infatuation—for that was all it could be—needed to cease immediately.

Ah, but look at how her smile sparkled once more!

He really must return to London. The country air had left him addle-brained.

"Thank you for saying so," Miss Elmsley said, her voice barely above a whisper.

Miles nodded, but kept his mouth shut. If he opened it, there was no telling what ridiculous words would fly out before his good sense could corral them back to where they belonged.

"Then you will attend tonight's ball?" Mr. Farthing asked, drawing Miss Elmsley's attention away from Miles, taking with it the warmth he had not realized it carried.

"Please, do, Miss Elmsley," Lady Charlotte said, offering her encouragement.

With one last fleeting glance toward Miles, Miss Elmsley gave a definitive nod and set her shoulders back as if she were about to march into battle. "Very well then. I shall brave the masses and attend tonight's party."

Miles forced a smile, but inside, need and want waged against each other for the upper hand. While he needed to restore his family's reputation by marrying the likes of Lady Charlotte, what he wanted…

Oh, hell, what he wanted was the woman sitting to his right! There, he'd said it. Furthermore, he wanted her in a way that defied all logic or good sense or propriety. In fact, there was nothing even remotely proper about his feelings for Miss Elmsley.

Not one bloody thing.

CHAPTER EIGHT

"I'm pleased you changed your mind about attending this evening," Mr. Farthing said as he escorted Patience around the perimeter of the ballroom. "I only wish I had been the one to convince you. I take it you and Lord Walkerton are friends?"

The manner in which he stressed *friends* caught Patience's attention. She did not like it. It was as if something lingered behind the question, a veiled meaning that said more than the actual word indicated. The crush of the ballroom was as thick as it had been the night she'd toppled Mr. Butterfield and Lady Mertle like dominos, but unlike that evening, tonight she was determined to be on her best behavior. She would keep her temperament even, with no spikes of anger to send her marching out of the arms of a gentleman and straight into disaster.

So instead, she only smiled and said, "Friends? Why do you ask?"

Mr. Farthing continued to smile down at her, his blue eyes soft and guileless, though if Patience wasn't mistaken, something more lurked behind them. An essence she couldn't quite put her finger on or determine whether it made him friend or foe.

"It is just that given the gravity with which you gave his suggestions over mine, I assume the two of you have been long acquainted. I must admit, I am a bit wounded you did not feel my urgings for you to attend were of the same level of importance."

Patience glanced up at Mr. Farthing, unsure if he was teasing her or not. It was difficult to tell. Though his smile held firm, the slight twist of his lips gave the impression he was a bit put out over the favoritism she had shown Lord Walkerton.

"You and I have only just met, Mr. Farthing. Lord Walkerton and I have been acquainted for a few years now. I suppose it is only natural then, that I would give his words more weight. Do not take it personally."

"Are the two of you particular friends?"

And there it was again. That sense, the way he stressed the word *particular* that raised the hackles on the back of her neck. As if he inferred something untoward. Salacious almost. Though, again, the expression on his face gave little indication that was what he meant. Perhaps she was being oversensitive. The only salacious part of her association with Lord Walkerton was the annoying and rather troublesome thoughts of him that kept entering her head at the worst possible moments. Thoughts that had her wondering what it would be like to make him smile on a regular basis. Or to kiss those lovely lips as he smiled. Maybe kiss them and *make* him smile.

"You are smiling, Miss Elmsley," Mr. Farthing pointed out, one blond eyebrow arched upward.

She stopped smiling and set her mouth into a prim line. "Lord Walkerton and I are acquaintances and nothing more."

"Good," he said, tucking her arm a little tighter beneath his as they turned a corner on the outer edges of the ballroom floor. "I am most pleased to hear that. I should hate to think I must compete for your affections with a titled gentleman. I would be well out of my league."

His claim startled her, his words tangling around her feet and causing her to stumble. "Compete for my affections?" Just repeating such made her squirm with discomfort. Yes, Mr. Farthing was a nice gentleman, and good looking as well, no question. Several ladies had commented on such this evening. And he certainly appeared to enjoy himself and take life none too seriously, the complete antithesis of Lord Walkerton, who did not appear to enjoy anything that she could tell. But—

But what?

She sighed. But he was *not* Lord Walkerton and for reasons she could not fathom, her heart had begun to attach itself to the taciturn earl and refused to let go. It was almost as if her heart had determined she must wrest him from his dour disposition and teach him to smile and laugh and enjoy life, instead of treating it like an event that must be endured.

"Should I take your silence as an indication that I am out of my league?"

Mr. Farthing's question brought her back to the present moment and she gave her head a small shake to free it of thoughts of Lord Walkerton. Such imaginings, while quite pleasant, would come to naught.

"Not at all, Mr. Farthing. I simply wasn't aware of your…intentions in that regard." Her face flamed, a rather disconcerting event given her pale skin made it impossible to hide. "We have barely known each other more than a handful of days."

"Then would it be too soon to request you call me Anton? Given we are living under the same roof and I am a certain friend of the family, I do not think your family would mind, do you?"

"Oh." Perhaps Mother would not, but Uncle Arran and Father might have a different opinion on that account. As for her, the idea made her a bit uncomfortable. "Uh…I…well, that is to say—"

Mr. Farthing shook his head and shot her an apologetic look as they completed their circle around the room. "I have been too forward, haven't I? My humblest apologies, Miss Elmsley. I've been away from proper society too long due to my time in the military."

"Do not trouble yourself, Mr. Farthing. I am hardly one to take someone to task over a slight gaffe, hm?" Patience smiled, thankful to have their conversation back on even footing.

Mr. Farthing was a handsome man and Uncle Arran allowed that the man's father was of impeccable character and well thought of. And Mr. Farthing did not seem the least bit put out by the notion that her own reputation was somewhat tarnished by behaviors attributed to letting action get ahead of good sense.

What had Lord Walkerton referred to it as? *Impulsive behaviors.* Yes, that was it.

Oh, bother, there she went thinking of his lordship again. She must stop this, for as soon as her thoughts traipsed off in that direction her gaze followed, searching through the bodies present to find his dark hair and hazel eyes within the crowded ballroom.

She dropped her gaze to the floor. She would not look. Lord Walkerton had been kind enough to encourage her to attend and not hide away, and for that, she was thankful. It was a quiet acknowledgement that perhaps the event that had sent her fleeing was not entirely upon her shoulders. But she must not read more into his admission than that.

Still, the way he'd gazed at her on the sleigh ride had done something to her insides that left her most unsettled. It was as if his gaze had reached in and touched her heart, set a brief kiss upon it that quickly settled in as if it had found a home. Which was ridiculous and further proof that she had lost her mind, because the last thing Lord Walkerton wanted was to kiss her. Not her heart, not her lips, not any other part of her she could name.

And she could name quite a few because such scandalous thoughts had kept her up to all hours of the night and forced a deep ache to develop between her legs that made finding sleep most difficult.

"Miss Elmsley. I am pleased to see you in attendance."

Patience looked up from the parquet design beneath the edge of her gown to find the object of her thoughts. How did he do that? Pop up out of thin air whenever she allowed her mind to wander in his direction. It was as if her thoughts had conjured him up.

"Lord Walkerton. I had not—that is to say—hello. I mean good evening. H-how lovely to see you." Her tongue entangled about itself, fanning the flames of the blush that had cropped up earlier until her cheeks burned.

Lord Walkerton inclined his head then turned the power of his gaze to Mr. Farthing.

"I meant to ask you, Mr. Farthing, you indicated you were in the army, yet you do not go by any rank. Why is that?"

Mr. Farthing said nothing for a brief second then smiled, though the expression appeared insincere. "I was a Lieutenant, though as I have recently returned to civilian life, I prefer to leave such matters behind." Another smile, though something about it appeared forced to Patience. The tightness about the edges perhaps, or the flinty spark in his light blue eyes.

"Ah," was all Lord Walkerton said in reply, giving little away as to what he thought of Mr. Farthing's decision. An awkward silence descended upon them as the two men stared at one another.

Patience shifted and cleared her throat. "And are you enjoying yourself this evening, my lord?"

"I have only just arrived," he said, turning his gaze to her where it warmed slightly and she had a lovely view of the kaleidoscope of colors that filled his irises. Green and brown with shards of amber she found most mesmerizing. "Perhaps it will improve if you will agree to dance with me. A waltz perhaps?"

"Are you certain you wish to do so? It did not go so well the last time," Patience reminded him, offering him an out she sorely hoped he would not take. Being held in his arms was pure heaven. At least it had been until he had claimed her a constant irritation. Though, in fairness to Lord Walkerton, she had been the one to ask the question.

Perhaps, in future, she should avoid making inquiries into subjects she did not really want the answer to.

"I am willing to make the attempt if you are."

She should say no. This could come to no good, these ridiculous feelings Lord Walkerton invoked in her. The last thing she needed was to entertain the notion they had any kind of a future together. He had made it perfectly clear the type of wife he wished for and save for being female, she did not fit any of his chosen categories.

Except when she opened her mouth to decline, Lord Walkerton smiled at her. Not a big smile, but a genuine one nonetheless, and the expression made her tingle from head to toe, wrapping her in a warmth that spread throughout and a different answer tripped off her tongue with ease.

"I am most willing, my lord."

"I am most willing, my lord."

Miles closed his eyes and pinched the bridge of his nose. It had been hours since Miss Elmsley had offered up those words and he'd held her in his arms, waltzing about the ballroom barely feeling the floor beneath him. Hours since he had been entranced by her smile and the sparkle in her eye. Hours since he had returned to his bedchamber only to discover sleep to be an elusive bedmate.

Yet, only moments since the realization that the bedmate he wished to join him was a certain lady with a somewhat tarnished reputation and a penchant for embarrassing herself with her impulsive behavior.

"I am most willing, my lord."

Despite the innocence of her words, the seductive promise of them made it difficult to keep the tantalizing images of what he wished they meant at bay. They resonated in his mind and while their waltz did not end in disaster this time, it might well have had the music endured a moment longer. That fault would have been his. He had been unable to help himself from pulling Miss Elmsley closer with each turn about the floor until their bodies almost touched by the time the last note played.

And, Lord help him, he'd wanted their bodies to touch.

"Bloody, bloody hell!"

Miles threw back the blankets and stalked to the window, but the cool air did little to tamp down the burning ardor in his veins for a woman he simply could not have. He needed to put this ridiculous infatuation to bed.

No! Not to bed. To rest.

He groaned and drove his fingers through his hair, clenching handfuls at the back of his head. What was wrong with him? Where had things gone so far afield from what he'd intended when he came to Sheridan Park? He'd had a plan. Improve relations with his brother and find a suitable bride.

Actions he'd dedicated himself to, yet in the course of a week, this slip of a woman had completely tossed him off his path with little more than a smile.

But it wasn't just the smile, was it? It was the question. That damnable question that continuously echoed inside of him as if she had just uttered it.

"What of love and laughter and silliness and fun? Do you not wish for any of those things?"

Naturally, he had scoffed at her suggestion. Claimed such things to be trivial. What place did any of those things have in his life? What place had they ever had? None. Nor had he expected that to change.

Except that it had. Somehow. Her words had infiltrated the barriers he'd placed about his heart, seeped into his consciousness, and burrowed deep within his soul, creating a profound longing without truly knowing exactly what it was he longed for.

But one thing he did know with an alarming certainty—if he wished to have any of those things, then he must take Miss Elmsley with them. And that idea was fraught with peril. He had spent his life, from his earliest memories, attempting to control his environment. To mitigate the damage done by his father. To be better. To be perfect. Was he now to toss all that aside? Destroy the progress he had made?

His mother would pitch a fit and likely denounce the match for all she was worth. She was already pushing for him to speak to Lady Charlotte's uncle, using Miss Elmsley's tumble of earlier in the week as an example of the type of woman he should avoid at all costs. The type of woman who would bring further stain upon the family name and the title he now bore.

The idea of giving up everything he had worked toward left him at odds. If he was not working toward this goal, what was his purpose? What value did he hold? None. Had this not been proven time and again? His own father had barely acknowledged him unless it was to scoff at him, tell him he was too *tightly wound*. His mother had never shown him an ounce of maternal affection, instead lavishing him with constant criticism and discontent. Even Lady Rebecca and Lady Henrietta had rejected him in favor of other men. Better men.

No matter how hard he tried to make things better, to do the right thing, nothing ever improved. His father's past actions would never change. His mother's misery was so ingrained she treated it as if it were her birthright.

Only Miss Elmsley appeared less interested in his title or fortune and more concerned with his happiness. As if it mattered.

As if *he* mattered. As a person. As something beyond a title and a fortune and a familial history.

Miles pulled aside the heavy curtain and looked out the window into the night. It had snowed earlier in the evening, leaving behind a pristine blanket of white upon the rolling hills that sparkled in the moonlight.

Was it worth exploring, this idea that there was more to marriage than duty? Marcus certainly thought so, and from the looks of many of the other lords and ladies packed into Sheridan Park for the yuletide, his brother was not alone in that thinking.

Miles stared at the landscape beyond the window and breathed it in, letting its beauty flow beyond his vision into the empty spaces that lived within. Then he closed his eyes to hold the sensation inside of him, but it wasn't the landscape that lived in his mind's eye. It was, as he expected it would be, Miss Elmsley, with her smile and her sparkle and her promise of a life worth living.

And Miles could not help but smile in return and allow the inkling of possibility to grow, along with the warmth her image kindled within him.

What if...?

He opened his eyes and let his gaze drift back to the empty bed.

What if, indeed.

CHAPTER NINE

"Come now, Callum, surely you can throw straighter than that!"

Patience laughed and ducked behind the barricade she had built up around a fallen tree as her ten-year-old cousin threw another snowball. It fell short, hitting the tree and sending a spray of flakes over her face.

"That's jus' a warnin' shot, lassie! Next one will hit the mark for sure!" Callum may have spent the last year in England, but his native brogue was alive and well and the cadence of it always reminded Patience of home. Though her father was English through and through, the Sutherland side of her family was as Scottish as they came and fiercely proud of their heritage, no matter how long they had spent on English soil.

"Oh dear," Patience laughed. "I've awakened the beast. I've heard a Scotsman never takes a challenge lightly."

In response, another snowball hit the tree, this one closer than the last. "Take that, English!"

Patience let out a short squeal and ducked, laying flat against the snow covered ground so the cold

seeped beneath her wool coat. Challenging Callum
to a snowball fight had been exactly what she had
needed to escape from her thoughts and from
constantly being on guard against doing anything
foolish that would embarrass her family. It was
difficult to allow thoughts of Lord Walkerton to
occupy her mind when she had to constantly bob
and weave to avoid being hit by Callum's hard-
packed pellets of snow. How refreshing not to have
to worry about propriety and etiquette and all that
silliness. Here, with Callum, she could just be
herself, away from judging eyes and free from the
whispered gossip she so often incurred.

Patience maneuvered herself to a thicker spot of
the tree to offer her better protection. She had been
stockpiling her snowballs and now it was time to
strike the little imp back with the full force of her
arsenal.

She filled her arm with her perfectly shaped
snowball then jumped up and began throwing them
one after the other. "Take that you rascally Scot! I'll
never give up my—"

"Bloody hell!"

"Oh! Good heavens!"

The remaining snowballs fell from Patience's
arms as her hands flew to her mouth in shock.
Callum's head popped from his own self-made
fortress of snow, shock written across his youthful
face mixed with a mischievous hint of amusement.

"Well done, Patience, you've taken out your own
countryman."

And indeed, she had. Laughter bubbled up from
deep within as Lord Walkerton slowly unbent from

where he'd attempted to curl into himself and protect his head from the worst of her assault.

"Oh, dear. My humblest of apologies, my lord."

Lord Walkerton brushed slowly at the spots where snow stuck to his well-cut wool outer coat, its color as dark as his hair. "Your apology would have a more authentic ring of sincerity to it, were you not laughing while you issued it," he pointed out in that stern tone she heard far too often.

"Would it?" She tried to control herself, but heavens, he made an amusing spectacle spotted with the remnants of her ammunition.

"Indeed. And I find your lack of sincerity most distressing. This behavior of yours is completely unacceptable and I have no other option but to take you to task for it."

"Is that so?" Oh bother, was he about to get sanctimonious on her when they were only having a bit of fun? Such a killjoy. And after last night's dance where he had pulled her closer as they waltzed, she had hoped they had turned a corner. That he had stopped expecting her to fit into a tidy mold of the perfect little lady and accepted her as she was. Flawed but well-meaning. Apparently, she had been mistaken—

"Oh!" A snowball pelted the fallen tree directly in front of where she stood, sending its shrapnel flying upward to splatter against her coat.

Patience glanced up from the attack, her eyes widening as she witnessed Lord Walkerton shaping another snowball in his gloved hands. Behind him, Callum was laughing loud enough to be heard clear across the way to Havelock Manor.

"As I said, Miss Elmsley, you must pay for your insolence."

Patience stood and stared at him. Because he had smiled as he issued his decree. Not completely. Just one side of his mouth had turned upward in a knowing smirk, but blessed be if that wasn't all it took to wake the nest of butterflies in her belly until they batted their wings, demanding release. But the butterflies must wait because it appeared as if Lord Walkerton fully intended to—

She hit the ground before the next snowball landed, sailing over her to land in her stockpile of ammunition, destroying several. "Why, you turncoat!"

She stayed behind her tree barrier for a few brief moments, considering the idea that Callum had hit her in the head, bringing on a delirium where she imagined Lord Walkerton having fun. But the laughter from the other side of the fallen log that protected her, told her otherwise.

She shook her head, bits of snow falling from the curls that had come loose from her hat. How could this be?

But there was no time to ruminate. She was under attack and, despite being outnumbered, she refused to go down without a fight. After exchanging several volleys, she pulled herself closer to her stockpile and slipped the knitted hat from her head, filling it with her perfectly packed snowballs. Then, in one swift motion, she stood and swung the hat about her head a few times before letting it loose. As the hat flew across the neutral space between the warring parties, the snowballs fell out, raining down upon the enemy who had quietly been creeping up on her.

"Ah!"

"Balls, the snow went down my back!"

"Language, young man. There is a lady present."

Patience threw two more missiles in quick succession and was rewarded with Lord Walkerton's desperate decree: "Retreat, retreat!"

"We've nowhere to go but open space!"

Patience laughed as Callum and Lord Walkerton ran back behind the safety of their barricade, though most of her merriment came not from her victory, but from the sound of Lord Walkerton doing something completely out of character.

Having fun. Laughing. It was almost inconceivable. Perhaps he was the one who had been hit on the head. Regardless, she had never heard a more joyous sound, and the desire to hear it again, up close, to see the effects of his smile etched into the familiar features of his handsome face became too overwhelming to resist.

"Do you wish to call a truce?" She yelled from the safety of her log fortress.

"She's fully stocked, my lord," Callum said. "And we're out of supplies. I've picked the area clean. Truce may be our only hope."

"Solid advice, young man. I feel I may have to promote you to the rank of general after this."

"But we lost the battle, sir."

"Ah, but we live to fight another day." Lord Walkerton's voice grew louder as he called over to her. "Very well, Miss Elmsley, what are the terms of surrender?"

Patience pushed herself up to her knees and peered across the short distance separating their camps. Lord Walkerton's hair was mussed and his cheeks reddened from the cold and the exertion of his campaign, but most of all—he was smiling. Broadly and freely as if he were experiencing the time of his life. Good heavens. How was it that the warmth of his smile didn't set all the snow around them to melting? Such power it had. For a brief moment, Patience could not remember what he had asked her.

"I'm a wee bit famished, Patience, if we could perhaps come to terms sooner rather than later," Callum suggested, which was not news to anyone who knew the boy. Patience swore he ate his own weight in sustenance each day, yet it never showed on his frame. She suspected he would grow to be like Uncle Arran, tall, lean, and strong as an ox.

"I suggest we reconvene at the main house. Cook has a pot of cider simmering on the stove. Or warm chocolate if you prefer, my lord. And biscuits. I do not like to leave my prisoners under fed. Very bad sportsmanship, I think. Should you escort me home, I shall grant you your freedom in due course."

Callum and Lord Walkerton looked at each other and Lord Walkerton nodded. "It seems a fair exchange. Could you be a bit more specific on how long this due course might last?"

Patience shrugged. "I suppose I shall let you go in time to enjoy this evening's entertainments. I understand there is to be a musicale of sorts tonight. Someone has foolishly convinced Judith and Benedict to reenact their duet from last Season."

"Ah, yes. I've heard stories of that event. Perhaps we could remain imprisoned until after that particular performance."

Patience laughed, surprised at how easily humor came to Lord Walkerton when he wasn't trying his hardest to be serious and proper. She liked this version of him. She liked it a lot.

"Unfortunately, I cannot. If I am to suffer through it, so must you. Now come, we have our horses over here." She nodded toward the wooded pathway that led to Havelock Manor where they had hobbled their horses near a patch of exposed grass.

Lord Walkerton made his way through the snow, picking up the reins of the horse he'd left a little ways off and joining them near the pathway. What a fine figure he cut—the darkness of his lean build against the unspoiled snow. She took in a deep breath and let it out. Callum raised an eyebrow though thankfully, kept his thoughts to himself as he mounted his horse and guided it toward the well-trod path.

When Lord Walkerton reached her, he looped the reins around the pommel of his horse and came to stand next to her. "Shall I provide some assistance?" he asked. The smile he'd worn earlier had lessened, but the remnants continued to linger around the edges of his mouth and in the sparkle of his hazel eyes. My, he had such lovely eyes, the mix of color creating an intoxicating blend of brown, green, and amber. And that dimple. Its appearance was like unwrapping a present and finding the most unique treasure hidden inside.

"I would be most pleased if you did so." Though in truth, Patience could have easily settled herself sidesaddle without help. One did not grow up with a brother like Charlie without learning a little self-sufficiency. But the thought of having Lord Walkerton's hands about her waist once more was too intoxicating a prospect to pass up.

He smiled at her, but made no move to lift her up and her body itched for him to do so. To feel his touch even through the heavy coat and layers of wool and petticoats beneath. "I do not believe I have ever taken part in such a spirited contest, Miss Elmsley—"

"Patience." She didn't mean to interrupt, but she suddenly wished to hear her name upon his lips.

"That would be improper."

"My good sir, you have thrown snowballs at me in the middle of a field where our only chaperone is a young boy of questionable repute." She could not help but smile as his eyes widened over the reality of their situation. "I am afraid to tell you that proper was never in attendance here today and I do not think it is required to show up now and ruin all the fun. Besides, as your captor, you are under my command until I release you and therefore must do as I say."

"A very dangerous turn of events if ever there was one." The worry that had flared up in his eyes disappeared, chased away by his smile and the sudden glint in his eyes that suggested their situation did not bother him anywhere near as much as she might have expected. "Very well then, *Patience*. I thank you for a most entertaining afternoon."

"Now, was that so hard, Miles?" She turned his name over on her tongue, traces of its taste remaining even after she'd spoken it.

Something in his expression altered, looking both hopeful and pained all in the same instance. "A little." Another smile. Goodness, she would never tire of seeing that. Without another word, he lifted his hand and brushed a finger over the tip of her nose. "Snow," he said, by way of an explanation, his gaze delving into hers until its potency rushed through her limbs and a few other places that should have concerned her but didn't.

He was going to kiss her. She could feel it. Like lightning in the air, it crackled around them. Heavens, but how she wanted him to do so! She leaned in a little closer and her eyelids began to flutter closed in anticipation.

"Are you two coming or are you going to stare at each other with cow eyes all bloody afternoon while I sit 'ere starving to my death?"

They jerked apart and Patience bumped into her horse, who snorted its disapproval. Miles looked as shocked as she was disappointed, though there was a hint around the edges of his expression that hinted at relief that Callum had rescued him in the nick of time from a horrible gaffe. She should feel the same, but she didn't. She had wanted that kiss. She still did.

"Language, young man," Lord Walkerton called out, but his gaze remained fixed on hers while the briefest glimmer of a suddenly shy smile returned to his lips. It was as if he wasn't sure how to act toward her now that he had almost kissed her. "I fear for that boy's future."

Patience forced a smile of her own and picked up the conversation to cover her hurt at his lack of disappointment over the untimely interruption. As it turned out, ten-year-old boys were very effective chaperones after all.

"I don't. He's a special lad with his father's sharp mind and his late mother's generosity. He'll do just fine." If she didn't smother him in his sleep first for robbing her of the experience of kissing Lord Walkerton. Miles. Such a lovely name.

"And where is it that he gets his penchant for swearing?"

"Oh, well, that comes from Charlie, of course. Now," she turned her back, the edges of her smile beginning to ache as she held it in place. "Give me a hand up, my lord, before the poor lad withers from starvation."

Miles enjoyed the sound of her name on his tongue. *Patience*. It held a lovely softness to it, a pleasant ease that belied the meaning of the word. Or the fact that it had to be applied to its owner on a regular basis or one might lose their mind a little.

Though, it was a bit late for that, wasn't it? Clearly, he had already lost his. The fact he had almost kissed her in full view of her cousin was proof of that. Good heavens, what had he been thinking? But he hadn't been, had he? No. He'd been too busy feeling. Too busy falling into her sparkling blue eyes and warm, inviting smile to remember the multitude of reasons he should not allow this to happen. He'd brushed the snow from the tip of her nose as an excuse to touch her, even though it was but a tease as his gloves kept him from feeling the soft skin dotted with pale freckles.

She was a wonder to him. She had been since the first moment he'd become aware of her, dumping punch over Lady Susan's head because the woman had slighted her cousin. And in the time that followed, the more he came to know her, the more he realized what a dangerous combination she was. Joy and frivolity and gregariousness all bundled together in a winsome package that enticed and intoxicated and embodied everything he needed to avoid. Yet, since the moment she'd settled herself into his carriage in London a fortnight ago, he had not been able to stop thinking of her. Or wanting her. Or needing her.

She'd bewitched him completely and he had no defense against it.

Against her.

When she'd invited him to Havelock Manor for hot cider, he should have made his excuses, but he did not wish to. No matter how logical it was for him to turn tail and run. He wanted to soak up every last minute he could, because soon it would end. Soon, he would be catapulted back into his regular life filled with his mother's carping, the expectations of mitigating his father's past actions, and his own need to prove he was nothing like the man who had sired him. And the joy and happiness he'd experienced this afternoon would become nothing more but a distant memory.

At least, it had been joyful and happy until *he* had shown up.

Miles had conveniently forgotten that Mr. Farthing was in residence at Havelock Manor. When the man entered the sitting room where Miles visited with Lady Elmsley and Patience, the previously sweet tasting cider had turned tart on his tongue.

Anton Farthing grated.

Miles couldn't say exactly what it was about the man in particular that wore on his nerves, but there was something…shifty about him. As if an ulterior agenda lurked beneath the pasted on smile and overly pronounced manners. Though, if Patience and Lady Elmsley saw anything false in his manner, he could not detect it. In fact, Lady Elmsley welcomed Mr. Farthing with as much enthusiasm as she had he, and he was an earl! One would think that would endear him more to the baroness, but it did not appear to. Nor did it appear to mean anything to Patience, either.

And why should it? It wasn't as if he planned to court her. He'd made that perfectly clear, hadn't he? The picture of the perfect wife he'd painted for Patience was the antithesis of everything she was. And yet…

He sighed and watched the easy discourse between the three as they chatted about the upcoming party that evening.

Miles could have sworn when he'd almost kissed Patience in the middle of the field that she had *wanted* him to do so. That she had shared his disappointment that Callum had interrupted them.

Marry her, Marcus had advised.

He shook the thought from his head. Mother had already set about berating him for dancing with her last evening, claiming he courted disaster in having any further association with a hoyden such as Patience.

But, oh, what a lovely disaster it would be.

He gritted his teeth against the image threatening to form in his mind. One of the snowballs that had smacked the back of his head and exploded into a shower of clumped flakes had obviously addled his brains. He could not marry Patience. Much as the thought appealed, he must do his duty. It was all he had. All he knew.

"Do you not think so, Lord Walkerton?" Farthing's voice interrupted his musings and he glared at the man, as if he alone was responsible for the fact that Miles had no idea what they were discussing.

"I'm certain I have no opinion on the matter," he said, hoping that would allow him to sidestep commenting on an unknown subject and looking like a fool.

"You have no opinion on whether I wear the blue or red dress?" A merry twinkle danced in Patience's eyes and a smile pulled at her lovely lips. How easy that expression came to her. How easy it was to fall into it as if nothing else in the world existed.

"I'm certain you will look lovely no matter which dress you choose."

His comment caused Lady Elmsley to lift one eyebrow skyward and he feared he had overstepped, but he let his answer stand without alteration or addition. It was the truth, and sometimes, the truth simply was what it was.

Besides, Patience was smiling at him and Mr. Farthing was scowling, so he could not fathom a better outcome.

"Well," he said, setting down his cup and saucer on the occasional table next to his seat and standing. "I should return to Sheridan Park before it becomes too dark to find my way. Am I released from your custody, Miss Elmsley?"

Patience smiled and stood and, in response, so did Mr. Farthing. "I suppose I must allow it. It would be rather disastrous if you became lost in the dark. It would mean one less dance partner for me and you know how I love to dance."

If only Miles could claim all of her dances. The thought of her being held in someone else's arms created an uncomfortable sensation in his gut. "Then I shall do my part to see you are not left standing on the sidelines. You will be sure and save me a dance?"

"I will indeed." Another smile, as if she had an endless supply stashed inside of her. "Now come, I shall escort you to the stables to keep you from stumbling off into parts unknown."

"I will join you," Mr. Farthing said. "I could stand to stretch my legs a bit."

Miles opened his mouth to protest, to claim the last few moments of Patience's company all to himself, but Lady Elmsley stood and spoke before he had the chance to.

"Actually, Mr. Farthing, I wondered if you might assist me with something. There is a box I cannot seem to reach and I believe you are just the height to do so. It is upstairs in the salon. Would you mind?"

Miles watched the false smile plaster itself across Farthing's face, but the irritation in his gaze told the real story. Lady Elmsley could easily have instructed one of the footmen to do the deed, given such tasks fell under their purvey. Still, what could Farthing do? He was here on Lady Elmsley's largesse, and given Sir Arran was in strict disagreement with his presence, Farthing traipsed upon thin ice. On the positive side of the matter, there was little doubt that should Mr. Farthing try anything untoward with respect to Patience, her uncle would not hesitate to introduce the man to an early death. Sir Arran Sutherland was not a man to be trifled with.

"Oh. Well, yes, of course. When I return from the stables I would be happy to assist—"

"No, no. I must have it now. I will need it to prepare for this evening's festivities and I really do not wish to delay." Lady Elmsley stood with her hands clasped in front of her stomach, her shoulders pulled back, reminding Miles of a general issuing an order, though her tone remained most agreeable.

Miles kept his own smile in check when Mr. Farthing cast a derisive glance in his direction, though he couldn't help one last parting comment. "Best not to keep the lady waiting, Mr. Farthing."

Once they had retrieved their hats and coats, they left for the stables.

"No maid for chaperone?" Miles asked, looking behind them.

Patience shrugged and tucked her hand beneath his arm as if it were the most natural place in the world for it to be. "We are but going to the stables, my lord. Besides, as strict as Mother is about following Society's rules of propriety in London, once home she relaxes somewhat. She is a Scot after all, and it is a well known fact that Sutherland women can take care of themselves well enough to walk to and from the stables."

"Given your ability to throw a snowball, I can attest to the truth in that belief."

Patience laughed and they fell into a comfortable silence. After a few moments, she looked up at him. "I do not think Mr. Farthing is overly impressed with you, my lord."

Amusement pulled at the corner of his mouth, something he found happening more and more often in her company. "I'm afraid I am not overly impressed with him."

"Oh? And why is that?" They entered the stables and she led the way to where the stable boy had taken his horse, easily picking it out from the others stabled there. Charlie had once mentioned to him that Patience was a consummate horsewoman, taking after their uncle in that regard. Sir Arran had a fine stable of horseflesh and Miles would love to spend some time with the man, getting a better look. But for now, all he could look at was the lovely creature who had released his arm and moved to stand in front of him.

"I do not think he has the best of intentions where you are concerned."

She laughed and his horse's ears twitched as if it found the musical notes most pleasing. Miles could commiserate. "You sound like Uncle Arran."

"Your uncle is a very astute man." He looked around. Where was the stable boy?

Patience leaned against the post that ran from floor to ceiling. "William must be out bringing the horses in from the field," she said, as if reading his mind. "And what do you believe Mr. Farthing's nefarious intentions to be?"

He walked toward her, stopping at a distance that was decidedly improper. "I believe he wishes to court you, with a view to improving his station through marriage."

"I see. And not because I am good enough in my own right for him to wish to marry me?"

"Of course you are," he quickly amended. "But he has only known you for less than a fortnight."

"And one cannot possibly find anything of interest in another within that time?" She gave him a pointed look as if she knew. As if the thoughts that had tumbled through his mind unbidden since their journey to Sheridan Park began were common knowledge.

He sidestepped her question. To answer would be akin to jumping into quicksand. She possessed a much nimbler mind than people credited her with. "I only mean to say that I do not think Mr. Farthing is thinking of anyone but himself at the moment and that you should take care not to walk into a situation with him that leaves you exposed."

She smiled, but did not appear to take his warning with any due seriousness. "I assure you, Mr. Farthing has thus far behaved in a most gentlemanly manner."

"To lull you into a false sense of security, no doubt."

Her eyebrows lifted and she laughed once more. "Good heavens, you paint a rather bleak picture of the man's character. I must wonder why he vexes you so much?"

Why, indeed? He'd asked himself the same question repeatedly and the answer always came back the same.

"Because—" He stopped. What was he to stay? That he did not want Mr. Farthing to have her? That he did not want *anyone* to have her save for himself. Which was ridiculous, because he could *not* have her. But, God help him, how he wanted to have her. Completely. Thoroughly. And without regret.

"Because?" she prompted.

Miles's heart hammered in his chest and blood rushed in his ears. He stood on the precipice of disaster. He could feel it. Sense its slippery edge. He'd lived his life in a state of heightened awareness, avoiding anything even remotely scandalous or improper, yet the thoughts firing through his head at this moment were the epitome of both those things.

Bloody hell! Where was the damn stable boy?

"Miles?"

He was falling. He was tumbling head over heels into a crevice so deep and dark there would be no clawing his way out of it. No rescue. No absolution. He needed to stop this. But he couldn't. He closed his eyes, praying for mercy, but none was to be found. He reached blindly for her, his glove slipping beneath the collar of her cloak to rest against the curve of her neck. And he pulled her to him, the way a man dying of thirst did a cool glass of water.

CHAPTER TEN

His lips were the most glorious thing. Soft and warm and intoxicating. Surely, this must be what it was like when one drank too much brandy. Her head was fuzzy and her heart pounded in her breast and every inch of her burned with a fire she had never experienced before. She wrapped her arms around Miles's waist, absorbing the strength of him while cursing the wool coat that created a barrier between them. She had heard stories of ladies taking a tumble in the hay with their lovers and always thought it an odd thing to do, but now she understood. They had been swept away. Inebriated from the passion they drank from their lover's lips.

Who would have believed the stodgy and proper Lord Walkerton could do such delightful things with his mouth? His tongue. Oh, good heavens! This was, without a doubt, the most sublime moment of her life and—

Miles pulled away from her, swiftly and without mercy. His hands dropped away as if scalded by the passion rushing through her. He blinked. Stared. His chest rose and fell. Patience saw all these things at once and yet everything moved as if time had slowed to a crawl.

He regretted his actions. It was written all over his handsome face. The skin against his cheekbones had pulled taut. The corners of his mouth turned downward in grim censure. His eyes—those lovely, mesmerizing eyes—filled with shock and dismay. If only she could reach out, tell him not to fret. Pull him back to her so he might kiss her again. And again. But she dared not. Any movement might break the spell that lingered around them and then she'd lose any chance of grasping hold of the moment and bringing it back to life.

"Miles—"

"No!" The word came harsh and unexpected and Patience jerked in response. Miles quickly held out a hand, palm facing her. "No." More gentle this time as he closed his eyes as if to collect himself.

"It was just a kiss." It was *not* just a kiss. It was a magical, mysterious event that had changed her forever. But telling him that was likely not the best way to go. He obviously did not share her opinion, if the look he gave her at her assessment was any indication.

It was a look he had given her many times over the course of their acquaintance. The one that implied he thought her mad. She offered him a smile in the hopes it would help. It did not. Miles lifted his hand to pinch the bridge of his nose, then covered his eyes as if he could block out whatever had happened.

"I—forgive me. I did not mean to—"

She did not let him finish. This moment, this kiss, had changed something. No, it had changed *everything.* She simply could not allow him to sweep their kiss under a rug as if out of sight would put it out of mind. "You did not mean to what?"

"I—" He stopped short, his hand falling away and his gaze resting upon her for a brief moment before he exhaled and shook his head. "I should not have kissed you."

"Then why did you?" He had never struck her as the type to do something meaninglessly.

"I don't know."

"Liar." The word was out before she could stop it and he looked as if she'd reached out and slapped him.

"I am not—"

"You are," she said, cutting him off. "You kissed me because some part of you wanted to and I think you at least owe me the courtesy of telling me why that is so. And why now you wish to deny those feelings."

His gaze hardened with frustration. "A true lady would let me deny such for both our sakes."

Patience lifted a brow. "A true lady would call you out for your brash behavior and demand you make proper recompense for comprising her pristine reputation."

She waited for the hint of disgust to ripple across his stark features at the idea of her forcing him to do such, but it did not come. Curious.

She took a step forward. "Lucky for you, I have no desire to force you into a situation you do not wish to be a part of. My standing in Society may be somewhat lackluster, for want of a better word, but I still have my dignity. And I can see only one way out of this situation."

The muscles in his shoulders tightened, pulling them back, his gaze instantly alert. "And that would be?"

She smiled. "You must kiss me once more."

A laugh barked out of him, filled with astonishment at her bold suggestion. "I beg your pardon?"

"Kiss me. And, if after this kiss, you do not feel anything for me, we shall leave the matter be and never mention it again. We shall walk away as friends and mark this up to nothing more than a momentary lapse of judgment and a miscalculation on both our parts."

He shook his head. "I cannot kiss you again."

She shrugged, though his instant refusal hurt. "Why ever not? You kissed me the first time without hesitation. I see no reason for you not to do it a second time, to be certain the kiss meant nothing. Unless, it did mean something. Did it?"

She held her breath but refused to look away. Refused to let him off the hook. Deep inside, her intuition insisted he needed to answer the question, that she demand he answer or he—no *they*—would never be free of this moment.

He avoided looking directly at her, dropping his gaze to the planked floor beneath their feet and the pieces of hay and grass and remnants of oats strewn about it. As much as she loved the hubbub of a London Season, it had always been the stable that remained her most favorite of places. It soothed her. Accepted her. The smell, the quiet, the calming presence of the animals. There were no expectations inside of these walls. No need to be anyone other than who she was. The horses did not judge. The barn cats did not care if she exhibited proper behavior. But now, every time she returned here, it would be this moment she remembered. Whatever answer Miles gave her would color her experience of this place forever after.

"Tell me the truth," she insisted, unable to keep a hint of desperation out of her voice "Whatever it may be, tell me the truth." She did not want her favorite place tainted by lies. "Why did you kiss me?"

Miles pulled his hand through his thick, dark hair, leaving temporary grooves and let his head hang for a moment before taking a deep breath and looking up. Looking at her. Into her. The breath he'd taken eased out of him and he shook his head in resignation.

"I kissed you because, despite all logic that insists you are completely wrong for me, something inside of me claims that you are not. I cannot think of another without your image crowding them out. You haunt both my waking and sleeping hours and every time I rest my eyes upon you, I crave the touch of your skin upon mine and—forgive me— the feel of your body beneath me. I want to drink in your kiss, bathe in the light of your smile, and dance to the sound of your laughter. I want to know what it is like to live as freely as you do and take each day as it comes, each moment, for that matter. I want all of these things, but I know if I chase after them, I will never be able to repair the damage my father did to our family name. I will never be free of the dark shadow he has plagued my family with and I will not drag you into the dark with me. I have already witnessed the way my mother can dim the light within you and I won't have it. You deserve better than that."

His words settled around her, sank deep inside of her, and touched her heart in a way nothing else ever had. He loved her. Oh, he hadn't said the actual words, but he had said so much more and the message was clear. He loved her. Hopelessly. Against his will. In complete negation of his better judgment. Yet, he believed that if he gave into his feelings, he would lose all hope of the one thing he had fought for his entire life. The one thing that had formed every decision he had ever made and turned him into the man who now stood before her.

The man she loved.

The realization hit hard and sudden. She loved him. Had for some time now. Why else would she care so deeply about his happiness? About wresting him from the grip of his self-imposed solitude where he held everyone and everything at arm's length? As if he believed to let himself enjoy anything would bring all his hard work crumbling down around him.

The way loving her would. Had he not just confirmed that?

"Oh." The word escaped on a sigh. It was a small response to such a significant admission.

He looked at her, surprised. "That is all you have to say? Have I actually left you speechless?"

She smiled but the motion took effort. She was unsure of what to do. Should she force him to leave behind his hope of removing the stain left by his father's horrible deeds? Rumor had it that the late earl had forced himself on any number of young women and left them ruined in body and mind. It was a horrible, horrible legacy. But it was not Miles's legacy.

"Do you truly believe that people gaze upon you and see your father? They do not. Your behavior, throughout your entire life, has been nothing short of exemplary."

"And should I deviate from that path, the first thing that will come to their minds is that, in the end, the apple did not fall far from the tree."

"That is not true!" How awful that he carried such a belief in his heart. Was it any wonder he watched every step he took as if one misstep would spell his doom? How long had this dictate been beaten into him? At how young an had he been burdened with it? "And even if a few did think this way, many others would stand up and call them out on their foolish assumption."

Miles spread his arms wide then dropped them to his sides. "Such as who? I have no close friends, very little family, and none interested in making a closer acquaintance."

"I am speaking of those who have attended the festivities at Sheridan Park. Lord and Lady Blackbourne, Lord and Lady Huntsleigh, Judith and Benedict, my family, Mr. Bowen and Lady Rebecca. Lord Hawksmoor and Madalene."

He shook his head in disagreement. "I am of no real importance to those people."

"If you were not important to them, you would not be here. They are a very close group, this much I can vouch for. They do not invite someone into their home unless that person has been deemed worthy of their friendship for one reason or another."

Which begged the question—what *had* been the reason for Mr. Bowen inviting Miles? She had never seen Miles interact with any of those she had mentioned, save for a casual conversation at a party or some such thing, Mr. Bowen included. He had courted Lady Rebecca once upon a time, but that ended rather abruptly. Hardly a reason for her now husband to issue an invitation. Yet, here Miles was.

"I must admit, though, I am surprised Mr. Bowen was the one to extend the invitation, given you once courted his wife. How is it that came about?" Patience asked.

"It is of no matter."

Her eyes widened. She caught the whiff of a secret. Saw it in the way he shifted his gaze away from her to rest on the stable door a few feet away. His horse snorted in response, as if it too had caught the scent.

"Yes, it is." She took a step closer, unsure why the answer was of importance, yet knowing that it was. Instinct insisted the answer formed part of the elusive explanation as to what drove Miles forward with his insistence that he be perfect. "What are you not telling me?"

"I cannot say."

"Why?"

He still had not returned his gaze to her. "Because it is not my story to tell."

The need to know, the sense that the answer unlocked something she had yet to figure out, pushed her onward. "If it has an effect on you, then it is your story as well and if you need someone to share it with, to unburden yourself, then I wish you would allow that person to be me."

"You don't understand."

"Then give me the opportunity to do so. Tell me." She reached out and took his hand, wishing their gloves did not keep her from the skin-to-skin contact she so desperately craved.

He pulled her hand and brought her to rest against his body, wrapping his arms around her and holding her there. Her head lay upon his chest and his scent, a mix of leather and sandalwood, enveloped the space around her. He was solid and warm and alive, his heart beating beneath her ear. She had never experienced such an intimate moment with anyone before. Not even the kiss they had shared only moments ago could compare. There was something about being held so that went beyond the physical, as if she were pouring her heart into his.

"It goes no farther than here?" He whispered the question into her hair. She had left her hat behind for the short walk to the stables, and while it had been cold on the edge of her ears, she was now thankful for her forgetfulness.

"Of course not."

"Marcus Bowen is my brother."

Shock rippled through her then settled down and the truth of his claim filled in the questions she had asked. There was a brief resemblance, the dark hair, the serious nature, but that was where it ended. Mr. Bowen was leaner, perhaps a shade taller and his eyes a different color that took the measure of everything he saw, astutely sizing it up, while Miles's gaze had a way of holding everything and everyone at arm's length.

"Patience?"

She gave herself a mental shake. "How did this come about?" But she knew the answer even before he gave it.

"My father. He forced himself upon Marcus's mother."

The horror of such, of knowing one's own father could be so despicable when such behavior ran counter to everything you believed in, she could not imagine.

"B-but how?" Mr. Bowen's mother had been an employee of Lord and Lady Ellesmere at their estate, Braemore, well north of London. How would the late Lord Walkerton ever have had access to the poor woman to inflict such a horrible fate upon her?

Miles hesitated before answering for a fleeting second. "It is a long story, and not a pretty one. Regardless, it is not spoken of and while Marcus does not consider my father to be of any familial significance to him at all, he has been kind enough to extend an olive branch in my direction. A sure sign that he inherited none of my father's attributes and all the strength of character of his mother."

Patience had never heard Miles speak with such heated passion. His reverence for Mr. Bowen and his disgust for his father pulsated from him as if it were a palpable thing she could reach out and touch. What torture it must be to know the man who sired you was such a despicable human being. To never be able to wrest yourself from the fact his blood flowed in your veins. But Miles was wrong about one thing.

Patience lifted her head to gaze up at him. She needed to make him understand. Time was running short. Soon, Mother would wonder what was taking so long and she could not risk her probing questions. Patience was many things, but a successful liar was not one of them.

"No one expects you will turn out like your father, Miles. The fact that you are embraced by Society and that the most well-revered lords and ladies of the ton have invited you to spend Christmas with their families is a sure sign of this."

"None of which absolves me of the disservice rested upon Marcus for my father's deeds. What my father did, set in motion a series of events that caused my brother to suffer hardships that I can never recompense him for."

"I do not think he wishes you to do so. If Mr. Bowen has extended you an olive branch, that is his way of telling you he does not hold you responsible for someone else's horrible deeds. You should accept this branch in the spirit in which it was offered and leave the past behind you."

Miles dropped his forehead to rest against hers and his fingers lightly traced the line of her jaw. For a moment, he stayed like that, the light touch of leather against her skin sending tendrils of desire shooting through her to pool low in her belly and then lower still. When he lifted his head, she expected him to straighten and step away, but instead he pressed his lips against hers, gently. Softly. Almost as if in apology, though for what, she could not determine. He would never have to apologize for kissing her. It was the most delightful thing she had ever experienced and she hoped to do so again and again and again.

But when his mouth lifted from hers, she sensed the resignation inside of him. The retreat to the familiar. The inability to believe he deserved anything better, simply because his father was a monster.

The need to protect her from becoming a part of it.

"Miles—" she whispered his name in desperation, but already he was shaking his head, cutting her off.

"No. I wish it could be different. I wish I could make you my bride, take you home and spend my days having you teach me how to laugh and my nights making you sigh with pleasure, I truly do." His gaze delved into hers and brought with it the depth of understanding that he meant every word he said. "But wishing does not make it so. And I will not drag you into the darkness with me. I will not risk seeing the light within you that shines with such brilliance diminished by living a life in the shadow of my father's reprehensible actions."

"But I want—"

He shook his head. "No. You do not. It is not a place anyone would want to be. But it is my place. My inheritance. I wish you happy. I wish you a wonderful life filled with laughter and family and that silliness you gave me a taste of earlier this afternoon. But I cannot give you that, and so I must let you go."

"Miles, this is ridiculous!" But he had already let her go. Stepped away. Put his barriers back into place.

"You must go. Your mother will have begun to wonder over your extended absence."

The defeat in his voice broke her heart. Shattered it as thoroughly as his rejection that they were meant to be together. Worse still, in doing so, he consigned himself to the very kind of life he had just warned her about.

"Then let her wonder. I cannot allow you to give up. You deserve so much more!"

He swallowed and the muscles in his jaw flexed, the only hint her words had any kind of effect. Otherwise, he had turned to granite. Hard, immovable. Resolute.

He walked past her to the stall housing his horse and reached for the bridle hanging next to it.

"I would beg you to please leave me now, Patience. If you have any kind feelings for me at all. This is difficult enough. Please." The pain in his voice, in the tightness of his shoulders that told her he held himself together through sheer force of will alone, cut into her like a jagged edge, leaving her heart in tatters.

She did not want to leave.

But what other option did she have?

She had used all of her reasoning. All of her persuasion and it had been for naught. Miles had chosen his course and he would not be swayed from it. Nor would he invite her to travel that path with him.

"My lord, forgive me!" William ran into the stable out of breath, crashing through the silence that had fallen upon them. "One of the mares got a bit cheeky and decided to jump the fence. We 'ad to run her down and coax her back."

Miles answered the young boy, but his words were lost to her. As it turned out, when a heart broke it made a rather deafening sound.

Patience forced her legs to move and soon was inside the warmth of Havelock Manor, though she remembered none of the journey that brought her there.

CHAPTER ELEVEN

"I have not seen you the past few days. Have you been hiding?"

Miles glanced up from the book in his lap to find his brother leaning casually in the doorway of one of Lady Blackbourne's many reading rooms, his legs crossed at the ankle. Though his posture indicated a casual air, his direct gaze gave the sense that he saw much and missed little. It was a bit unnerving. The only other person of Miles's acquaintance who paid him that level of attention was Patience and she had seen far more than Miles wished. It left him vulnerable. Aching.

"I suppose I was in need of some solitary pursuits." He did not want to risk running into Patience. To see the disappointment she must hold toward him reflected in her gaze. "I confess I do not often attend such extended gatherings."

The shenanigans that went on at such events created an invitation to scandal he preferred to avoid. Such as the temptation to sneak down the hallway to the room Patience had once occupied in the insane hope that she might have returned from

Havelock Manor to stay at Sheridan Park once more.

Marcus pushed away from the doorframe and walked into the room to join Miles where he sat facing the hearth. His brother sat and stretched out his legs toward the warmth of the flames.

"I often come here when I need a few moments of solitude, as well," he said.

"Do you get many moments of solitude?"

Marcus offered a rare but genuine smile, the expression of a truly contented man. A fissure of envy opened inside of Miles. "Not as many as I used to. But it is all relative."

"In what way?" Marcus Bowen was the most self-contained man Miles had ever met. The only person who came close in comparison was perhaps Lord Hawksmoor. No wonder the two men had struck up an unlikely friendship.

"What I have gained from the moments of chaos has proven most fulfilling and a change of perspective is never a bad thing. It opens one up."

Miles did not care to be opened up. Though it was a little too late for that. Patience had already torn him open and laid him bare, hadn't she? He dropped his gaze back to the book in his hand. He'd read none of it, the words swirling around in front of him while his mind continuously returned to the stables. To the kiss. To the glorious sensation of holding Patience against him. And the heart-shattering moment when he let her go. For good.

"I have the sense you've experienced a little of your own chaos since your arrival here," Marcus said.

"Have I?"

"Yes. And I suspect your particular chaos goes by the name of Miss Patience Elmsley. Have the two of you had a falling out?"

Miles glanced up, startled. His brother's ability to read him was downright uncanny. Where most people looked to see, Marcus looked to observe and Miles was learning those two things were intensely different animals.

He cleared his throat and closed the book. Did he dare tell his brother what weighed upon his mind? He had never had a confidante before. But was that not what brothers were for?

Marcus raised one dark eyebrow as if reading Miles's mind and it became apparent that he might as well confide in him, given the fact the man had already determined his problem and quite possibly had a viable solution.

"I am…that is to say… She—" He let out a harsh breath. What was there to say about Patience? How did he properly articulate his feelings for her? Or admit that in the end it did not matter, because he had already rejected her affections and boxed up his own to store away somewhere safe in the vain hope out of sight would be out of mind? And out of heart.

"Dear God, man. You have it quite bad, don't you?"

Miles glared at his newfound sibling, only to find him smiling back, amused. Amused! Miles's world was falling apart at the seams, his heart had been torn from his chest by his own doing, and he was slowly dying inside and all Marcus could do was—smile! Could it be any worse than that?

Marcus laughed, the corner of his eyes crinkling, and Miles discovered that yes, it could be worse.

"I am so glad you are amused by my pain."

The laughter stopped and the smile faded somewhat but warmth lingered in Marcus's gaze as if he actually cared about what Miles was feeling. This was a new experience for Miles. He wasn't quite sure what to do with it.

"Your pain is your own doing, but I think deep down you already know that. Yet, despite this knowledge, you are going to allow this chance at happiness to slip through your fingers. I find this to be the height of stupidity and confess it leaves me a bit baffled. I had not taken you for a stupid man. I will have to change my assessment in that regard."

Miles's mouth hung open. He had never been spoken to in such a way by anyone. Well, perhaps by Patience when she scoffed at his idea of what marriage should be based upon, or his claim that fun was overrated and whatever other nonsense he had spouted at her.

He straightened in his chair and affected the lordliest air he could muster. After all, his brother was but a mister and he was, after all, an earl. Shouldn't that afford him some type of social courtesy? Then again, every lord he knew revered Marcus as if he were of the highest ranking. "I have done what I must do."

"And what is that?"

"I have informed Miss Elmsley that we would never suit and therefore any thoughts she had about the two of us forming a union must be put from her mind."

The eyebrow rose again. He was truly quite adept at that. "And did you say it just like that?"

The muscles in his shoulder and back collapsed beneath the weight of the truth and he slumped in his chair. "No, not exactly." Instead, he'd confessed to her a host of truly inappropriate things he wished he could do to her, share with her. Images that had filled his days with longing and his nights with a lustful need, until he could think of little else.

"But in the end, this abject rejection of happiness and of Miss Elmsley was the gist of the conversation?"

His shoulders sagged. "More or less."

"And you left her with no misunderstanding that a pairing between the two of you would never happen?"

"None. I was quite clear."

Marcus's expression darkened. "And what, exactly, was the ridiculous reasoning you employed to bring about such an asinine conclusion?"

Bloody hell, could he not get at least a little support from his brother? "It was not asinine! I have a responsibility that you of all people should understand."

Marcus cocked his head to one side. "And what is it you think I should understand?"

"About our father!" Frustration drove Miles to his feet. He had done the right thing. He always did the bloody right thing! He had to.

"My father is Edmore Bowen and he has been dead for over two decades, so I cannot imagine what he has to do with any of your actions with respect to Miss Elmsley."

Miles gritted his teeth until his jaw ached. The late earl may have provided the seed that sired Marcus, but his brother did not consider the man as having any relevance in his life beyond that. He despised Miles's father with a level of hatred that very few understood. But Miles did and he shared his brother's feelings.

It was because of what the late earl had done to Marcus's mother and so many others, that Miles had spent his days walking such a straight line of propriety that his existence more closely resembled a tight wire act than an actual life. It was his duty to pay the penance for his father's actions out of deference for what others—including Marcus and his mother—had suffered. Did he not owe them that much at least? Did he not owe them the peace of mind in knowing that the hurt his father had caused would not be repeated by the next generation? That chapter was dead and gone, buried with the late earl.

"My father destroyed more lives than I care to know about. His despicable actions have left a stain on the Walkerton title, on the Radcliffe name. On my name." He pressed a hand against his chest. "If I am to have any hope in removing that, I must be flawless in my decisions. I must show Society that his behavior was an aberration not inherited by his offspring. I have been diligent in avoiding any and all scandal or impropriety and I will continue to do so in the choice of whom I marry. Given this, it is of utmost importance that the woman I choose is the epitome of respectability and decorum in body, mind, and soul."

"And you have no objection to marrying a woman you do not love simply because she fits a profile you have conjured in your mind as to what Society will find acceptable?"

He sounded just like Patience. "Yes, that is what I must do."

Marcus stood and gave Miles a long, steady look, filled with myriad emotions, disappointment being the heaviest contender.

"Then your father wins in the end, doesn't he?"

His brother's words cut deep. The way only the truth could.

"What other choice did he leave me?"

"The choices you make should never be dictated by that man. If you allow that, you might as well dig your own grave now, for you will be walking through life as if you were already buried in the grave next to him."

"How can you say that? After what you suffered at his hand. After what he did to your mother—" Miles stopped, unable to continue as guilt choked the words in his throat.

"What he did to my mother cannot be undone, but it is not your crime to wear."

Miles took a deep breath. "Had things been different—had you been my full brother—it would be you who inherited the title. You would have rank and family and position."

"I have a family," Marcus said, his voice hard and uncompromising. "I have a wife who loves me. I have children who will carry on after me. I have friends who are like brothers to me and the memory of a mother and father who embodied every essence of those titles, and now I have a brother as well. I do not wish to be an earl, or a duke, or even a knight. I am happy with who I am and where I reside in the grand scheme of things. I bear you no ill will nor do I hold you responsible for deeds committed by your father. He was a despicable human being, but that is not your burden to bear. Set it down, Miles. Leave it be. You've carried it long enough."

His brother's words pummeled him, broke down the walls of righteousness he had erected and erased the strictures and dictates he'd been raised to follow. He stood bare, unsure. Who was he without these things?

"I don't know what else to do." The confession slipped out of him.

Marcus stood to join him. "You might start with choosing happiness, something the bastard that sired us destroyed at every turn. You can choose to marry a woman you love instead of a woman you think you should."

"But I have to—"

Marcus grabbed Miles shoulders and shook him. "Wake up, man! No, you do not. Is it forgiveness you seek for crimes you did not commit? Then fine, I forgive you. But you must stop this ridiculous and misguided self-flagellation. Is that the kind of life you want for yourself? Wouldn't you prefer to be happy?"

Of course it wasn't the life he wanted. But he knew nothing else. His mother had beaten it into him with her verbal assaults for as long as he could remember. He had carried the weight of it on his shoulders his entire life. If he chose to turn away from this, to embrace the unknown, what guarantee did he have that he could create a happy life?

"I'm not sure I would recognize happiness if it walked up and introduced itself."

Marcus squeezed his shoulder. "If I'm not mistaken, brother, it already has."

The suggestion was spoken quietly, the treasured moniker settling over Miles with a rush of gratitude. Despite everything, Marcus recognized him as family, as a brother.

If any good could come of his father's horrendous actions, this was it.

Only a greedy man would wish for more.

Misery was an exhausting thing. It weighed you down until you felt as if you were carrying around two people instead of one. One being this horrible, empty shell whose hopes and dreams had been shattered into a thousand tiny pieces and the other the dead weight of the happy person you used to be. All Patience wanted was to crawl into bed and sleep until the pain lessened. Until she reached the point where she could draw a breath without it echoing in the hollow chamber where her heart used to be before Miles had torn it out and trampled it flat.

But she could not. After too many days of crying on Judith's shoulder over Miles's rejection of her affections, her cousin had insisted she grab hold of her dignity and throw herself back into the festivities of the Season. Had Judith not threatened to bodily haul her off her bed, dress her in the first thing she laid her hands on and forcibly push her out the door without so much as allowing her time to put a cold compress on her tear-swollen eyes or fix her hair, she would still be there.

But despite Judith's advice that donning her favorite wool dress and apple red pelisse might brighten her mood, Patience remained mired in despair. Her brain continued to ask questions for which her heart had no answers. She was adrift. Lost.

The sensation was unfamiliar territory for her and not a place she cared to stay, but she could not seem to find her way out.

Why had Miles kissed her? Why had he said all of those wonderful, decadent things of what he wished to do to her—with her—if he did not plan on marrying her and following through with them? Had he intended to cause her grievous pain? She didn't like to imagine him capable of such a thing, but what other purpose was served in his making those claims? The whole thing made her head ache. She should have stayed in her room. The beauty of the crisp winter day, sunshine glinting off the snow lining the pathway where it wound around the skating pond, escaped her. The effort of pretending she enjoyed herself was too taxing an endeavor to continue for much longer.

"Are you not feeling well, Patience?"

She glanced up at Mr. Farthing as they walked along the pathway, taking the offshoot that led to a small shed in the distance that housed an array of skates in all sizes. Mr. Farthing had taken to calling her Patience over the past few days, though only when they were well out of earshot of Uncle Arran or Charlie. They, much like Miles, did not care for their houseguest and had insisted he had overstayed his welcome. But Mother had stood firm that throwing the young man out before the holidays would be cruel. And so he stayed, though his presence was of no interest to Patience. She'd been too busy nursing a broken heart to take much notice.

She had not requested that Mr. Farthing call her by her given name, however, nor did she reciprocate in kind. In truth, she found the familiarity he assumed rather off-putting, but she did not possess the stamina to mount an argument against it today, so she let it slide and dropped her gaze back to her feet as they trudged along the packed snow.

"I suppose I am ready for the yuletide to draw to an end. All the hubbub has left me rather tired."

The hubbub being falling in love with a man who had no wish to marry her, despite the fact that he loved her. And he did. She was as certain of that as she was the sky above her glowed a brilliant blue. He simply did not love her *enough*. And that was the most heartbreaking part of all.

"Truly? I find the festivities most exhilarating. All the lords and ladies. I have made many acquaintances I would otherwise never have met. I believe it will go a long way to elevating my status now that I have returned to civilian life. Most have been very accepting of me, save, of course, for Lord Walkerton."

Miles's name caught her attention. "What do you mean?"

Mr. Farthing shrugged. "It is clear the man does not like me. I suppose it has something to do with my mentioning I had known his father."

"Many people knew the late Lord Walkerton. I do not see how that would be significant to his lordship." She did not want to speak about Miles.

"Yes, but I mean that I *knew* him. I knew of his...lifestyle, shall we say, for lack of a better term."

A chill that had nothing to do with the cold winter air, tripped down Patience's spine. "I am certain I do not know what you are referring to."

"Then allow me to enlighten you, if for no other reason than to protect you."

"Protect me? From what?"

"From becoming an innocent victim of the aberrant behavior passed down from father to son. I have grown quite fond of you, Patience, and I wish to protect you. To keep you safe."

His words skirted over her, forcing her mind to pull itself from the murk days of crying and self-pity had entrenched it in. She released his arm as they reached the shed and turned to face Mr. Farthing.

"Whatever are you talking about? I am not so sheltered I have not heard the rumors of the late earl's behavior but I can assure you that Lord Walkerton is nothing like his father. He is a good man. A respectable man that gives great weight to behaving the consummate gentleman. He would not hurt me, or any other woman." And despite the pain in her heart from his rejection, she believed her claim. He had not meant to hurt her. He was simply too blind to see another path than the one he'd spent his entire life walking. All because of the man Mr. Farthing now accused him of being like. The very suggestion was preposterous.

"How can one know?" Mr. Farthing asked. "The way he looks at you, his eyes hungry as if you were a meal and he a man starving for sustenance, I would not be surprised if he attempted to take advantage."

"Mr. Farthing, you go too far with your suppositions!" The conversation had reached the level of ridiculousness and she was too tired to embark on it. "And stop calling me by my given name. It is improper and I do not—"

Not too far behind them, a group of young men and women from the village laughed heartily, swallowing up her insistence for propriety with their burst of gaiety. The sound washed over Patience and created a deep longing. Had it really been only days since she too had experienced such highs? Funny how time slowed down, stretching itself out like a languorous cat when one experienced the depths of despair, yet sped up like a hummingbird and rushed past when happiness paid a call.

Mr. Farthing took her hands in his, holding them against his heart. "Forgive me. I meant no offense, my sweet. But I cannot help myself when I am with you. You have captivated me body and soul and I cannot imagine leaving here without knowing you feel the same way."

Patience recoiled at his fervent declaration and pulled at her hands but he held fast. Behind her, the chatter of the group moving down the pathway behind them grew closer.

"You take too many liberties, Mr. Farthing," she said, a warning tone she rarely used entering her voice. "Release me this instant. I do not share these feelings."

She gave a light tug, but he did not relinquish his hold.

Must she make a scene? Would no one come to her aid? She looked along the pathway. The group was still in the distance, too far to hear their conversation and Mr. Farthing blocked their view of her, making them unable to see he held her captive in his grip. In the other direction, coming around the pathway on the skating pond, she spied Miles. Perfect. If she caused a scene now, she would all but confirm his decision that she was not marriage material. And in doing so, destroy the foolish hope she held that if she could conduct herself in a proper fashion without incident, that maybe—just maybe— he might change his mind.

"I cannot help my feelings, Patience. And I confess, I have thought of little else but kissing you since I first laid eyes upon your pretty countenance."

"Mr. Farthing!" she hissed his name, glancing toward Miles. He had stopped walking now and stared at them. Though his body appeared rigid, he remained too far away for her to see his expression. And he too far to see her silent plea. Did she dare call out?

"I must believe you too have felt the spark between us, despite Lord Walkerton's interference. Why you have allowed him to distract you I cannot imagine, but clearly, he has no interest in furthering a courtship with you. You embarrass yourself by chasing after him so."

Mr. Farthing's words were like a slap to the face, drawing her attention back to him. Is that what others saw? What they believed?

"I am the man for you, Patience. And with your family name, my elevation in Society will be swift and beneficial. No one will question such a union. My father is well respected and your father but a baron. It is not expected that you would reach beyond that to marry an earl."

"I do not care to marry anyone. Mr. Farthing, I demand you stop this behavior immediately. People are taking notice and I do not wish to become a spectacle of attention." Her cheeks burned. The crowd behind them had come to a stop, their gazes watching like curious birds from a hundred feet away. If she called out, would they assist her?

Mr. Farthing followed her gaze and glanced over his shoulder. Any fleeting hope that realizing they had an audience would bring him to his senses evaporated when he turned back, a covetous smile spreading across his face and a propitious gleam in his eyes.

Patience opened her mouth to shout out for help, but the words were swallowed as his mouth crushed hers, pressing so hard her lips hurt. The hard, rough wood of the shed met her back as she stumbled backward and Mr. Farthing released her hand only to slip one beneath her pelisse and grab at her breast then fumble with the buttons that held her dress together. All of this happened in an instance and she froze. God help her, she froze, unable to adjust to what had suddenly happened. To make sense of it. To mount a proper defense.

Then anger rushed through her and the instructions Charlie had drilled into her head from the moment she entered Society came with it. Mr. Farthing was too tall for her knee to be able to reach his private areas, so she bit hard against his lip until his hand released her and he jumped back, his hand covering his injured mouth.

"How dare you," she hissed.

Patience quickly scuttled out from between Mr. Farthing and the shed, finding freedom in the open pathway. But there would be no freedom from the scandal of what had just occurred. Beyond the group of men and women from the village staring at them mouths agape, a few of the skaters on the pond beyond had also taken notice of them. And despite the truth of what had actually occurred, she could tell from their expressions, what they saw was something entirely different.

But worst of all, was Miles, standing in the distance. He'd left the path to cut through the snow but stopped at some point and now stood silent, staring directly at her. Though still too far away to read his exact expression, Patience could feel it. His disappointment reached across the brittle winter air and seeped deep into her heart.

She opened her mouth to call out. To explain that it wasn't what it looked like. The kiss had not been mutual, or invited, and definitely not wanted. But her voice arrested in her throat, because in the end, what did it matter? In the end, everyone who had witnessed what had occurred would tell a different version.

After all, she was the girl who created spectacle wherever she went, and this would simply be the icing on the cake, wouldn't it?

"Forgive me!" Mr. Farthing stared at her, his eyes wide, though his words lacked sincerity. "I—I lost myself. I did not mean to—I will make things right, of course."

But Patience had stopped listening. What did it matter what he said? What he did? She was ruined. Surely and completely. Any hope she'd had of winning Miles back, convincing him she could be what he wanted was gone.

She gathered her skirts in her hands and turned, running past the staring group who had proved no help at all, and kept going until she reached the main house. The last remnants of her hopes and dreams left behind to litter the pathway in her wake.

CHAPTER TWELVE

"Mr. Farthing has, of course, offered marriage." Patience's mother folded the linen napkin and placed it upon the table, her breakfast untouched.

A full day had passed since the incident, which her family had come to refer to it as. Mr. Farthing had left Havelock Manor and was currently residing at the White Ram Inn until the matter between them was settled. Settled how, did not particularly matter to Patience as she had wrapped herself in a welcomed numbness. It was easier that way. To not feel. A shame she had not discovered this before now. Perhaps she might have saved herself a world of hurt.

"I am in complete disagreement with this marriage," Uncle Arran, his hand hitting the table and causing the wood to reverberate. "I told you from the beginning Farthing was up to no good. I care little for his claim of being overcome with emotion and temporarily losing his head. Bollocks, I say!"

The only answer to her uncle's outburst was her father's rhythmic drumming of his fingers against the tablecloth.

"Is there nothing that can be done to rectify the situation other than having Patience marry Farthing?" Charlie asked. "Surely, if we explain that what occurred was something she neither invited nor wished for we can mollify most of those—"

"Whether they are mollified or not will not stop the whispers or gossip, and that is what will ruin her reputation beyond repair," Father said, his voice tired but steady. Patience felt his gaze upon her but did not lift hers to meet it. What was the point? All she would see was disappointment. Regret. "You will not be able to make a better match than Mr. Farthing at this point. No other gentleman of good quality will offer for you. This incident has closed those doors."

"But, Father, surely someone—"

"No, Charlie," Mother said. "No one. Perhaps if this had been the first incident we might hold out a small hope that the damage could be repaired, but…"

But it wasn't. It was simply the most recent in a long line of incidents. All of which would now be judged and weighed together.

Her father spoke. "Patience?"

She lifted her gaze from the table, the effort leaving her exhausted. "Yes?" Her voice came from far away as if she had answered from the other room.

"We will not insist that you marry Mr. Farthing if you are dead set against it, but you must understand that if you wish to have a husband, children, then this may be your only opportunity to do so. And you must do it swiftly. We cannot allow the incident to fester in the minds of others without answer. If we do, both you and your children will wear the stain of it for years to come. You know how cruel Society can be."

And she did. Had she not witnessed the cruelty the ton had delivered to those she cared for? Judith, the Laythams, Lord Hawksmoor, Lady Henrietta. Miles.

And now, staring down a future that might leave any children she had wearing the fallout from an incident she had no control over, she understood with a startling clarity, Miles's conviction to protect future generations from the damage his father had wrought.

"I will marry Mr. Farthing," she said, the words heavy upon her heart. She did not love him. At the moment, she did not even like him. But what choice did she have? Live the life of a spinster? Never know the joys of having a family of her own? Perhaps she would never forgive Mr. Farthing for what he had done, or maybe in time his plea that he had been overcome by emotion would soften her heart enough that she could accept her fate. Either way, her choice between the two painted a rather bleak picture of her future.

And ultimately, what did it matter who she married? She would not love them. It was nothing against them. It was simply the way things were. Miles was the man she loved. The only man she would ever love. She wished it wasn't true, but there was little she could do to change it. All efforts she'd made to shut that part of her heart away met with failure, the truth bleeding through every barrier she erected until she gave up trying.

If she hoped to find at least a small modicum of happiness in her future with children she could shift this love onto, then marriage was her only choice. And Mr. Farthing was her only option. She had resigned herself to this fact, though she looked upon it without happiness or joy.

Perhaps Miles was right in the end. Those things had no place in such a union.

"Are you certain, dear?" Her mother reached out and placed a hand over hers, sadness having crept into the lines around her eyes.

Patience nodded in response, unable to get the words out twice.

"I don't see why we can't leave for the White Ram Inn, beat down the man's door and give him his due," Huntsleigh said, the earl's pale blue eyes blazing with a fury not often witnessed in polite society. "Why did we allow him to get away?"

Miles sat in the chair near the hearth, the same one he had sat in when Marcus had joined him and all but called him an idiot for forgoing his feelings toward Patience. How he had come to be a part of this conversation that whirled around him as Lords Blackbourne, Huntsleigh, Glenmor, and Hawksmoor, as well as his brother, Marcus, discussed the matter, he wasn't quite sure. He had come here seeking solitude, to make some decisions, then suddenly the horde descended.

His conversation with Marcus had given him clarity, a perspective he'd been afraid to consider, fearful he would get his hopes up only to watch them fall apart in the end. But the more thought he gave the matter, the more he realized Marcus made valid points. After all, how many gentlemen of his acquaintance, most of who were in this room now, had held their own beliefs toward marriage and what should be, versus what was? And had each one of them not been proven wrong? And in adjusting their expectations, each in their own way had found the happiness they longed for with the women they loved. And not a one of them looked the worse for wear after doing so. If anything, they all appeared blissfully happy.

Take Lord Blackbourne for instance. He had been mired in scandal not more than a few years past. A repaired reputation should have been the farthest thing from his grasp, yet he had achieved such redemption. And Lord Hawksmoor? Why, the man shunned Society and held its members by the throat while running The Devil's Lair. Yet, here he was, happily married to the daughter of his steward and caring little what Society thought about it. Even Miles's brother, an untitled gentleman, had married the only daughter of the late Earl of Blackbourne.

Not a one of them was disrespected in Society for their pasts.

Had Patience been right? Had Miles given his father's crimes too heavy an importance in his life? And in doing so, did it not allow the man to reach beyond the grave and continue his destructive ways as Marcus had suggested?

Would embracing happiness not be the best revenge in the end? Was it possible love was the only thing that would erase the stain of his father's actions? For what better way to chase away the dark than with light?

God help him, but he'd been such a fool not to realize this sooner. Had he, perhaps he would have reached Patience in time to stop what had happened. To keep her from Farthing's clutches. The image of their kiss still burned through him like an angry fire and his hand fisted against the armrest of the chair. What he wouldn't give to wrap it around the man's throat. Maybe it was as Farthing claimed and he was truly smitten with Patience for reasons other than bettering his station—and why wouldn't he be? But to force his hand, and hers, in such a way as to solidify his claim sickened Miles.

He should have reacted sooner. The moment he saw them together, he should have marched through the knee-high snow and interrupted. But he'd hesitated. Fearful he had no place to so so, given what he had said to her. His foolish rejection of her heart. And his hesitation had proven her downfall—something he would never forgive himself for.

"We did not let Farthing get away," Marcus pointed out, drawing Miles's attention back to the conversation at hand.

"Bowen is right," Lord Glenmor said. "We sent him to the inn because if he continued living under the same roof as Sir Arran, we would likely be digging his body out of a snow bank come the spring thaw."

Miles was not opposed to that idea.

"Regardless," Huntsleigh said. "Do you mean to tell me, if we all put our weight and support behind Miss Elmsley that we cannot rectify the matter and allay any scandal it has caused?"

Lord Blackbourne ran his fingers through his ink black hair leaving deep grooves. "Our support may allow her to show her face in Society, but it will not promise that she will make a good match, or any match for that matter. Farthing's actions created such a spectacle in front of enough people to have long-reaching consequences. Many have indicated she appeared a willing participant."

"She was not," Marcus said, shooting Miles a glance.

Blackbourne nodded his agreement. "I believe you are correct. I have spoken to Farthing. While I believe he holds a certain infatuation with Miss Elmsley, I am also certain he is equally infatuated with moving above his station when they marry. He saw his opportunity and he took it. With great success, unfortunately."

"Marry?" Miles jumped up from his chair. Surely he had heard wrong. "When was this decided?"

Glenmor glanced his way. "Judith informed me this morning that Patience has agreed to Farthing's proposal."

Miles cut his hand through the air. "Absolutely not! That is the worst possible thing. We cannot allow this!"

The other men turned to stare at him.

"Why ever not?" Marcus asked.

Did he just smirk? Miles was certain he saw the man's mouth twitch at the corner. How could he possibly find this amusing? He knew how Miles felt about Patience, yet there he stood, feigning ignorance while the other gentlemen present stood waiting for his answer.

Miles let out a growl of frustration. Brothers!

"Because Miss Elmsley believes marriage should be filled with happiness and joy and—and silliness." Bloody hell, he sounded like an idiot. "She has indicated repeatedly to me that entering into marriage for any other reason is a recipe for unhappiness and not something she would ever be a part of. I cannot now believe her heart would allow her to make any other decision but to refuse Farthing's proposal."

He sounded like a raving lunatic.

Marcus grinned in earnest this time, a lopsided affair that Miles instantly wanted to smack off his face. "And yet she has accepted his proposal."

"Out of desperation!" That was the only explanation. "We cannot allow this."

"Did you have another solution?" Lord Hawksmoor asked then took a slow drink from his brandy, watching Miles over the glass's rim.

"I—" He stopped. Did he? Would she even consider him after his rejection of her affections that afternoon in the stables? She had her dignity, after all.

Blackbourne stepped forward. "I am leaving this day to procure a special license, Walkerton. If I am to put someone else's name upon it other than Mr. Anton Farthing, perhaps you might want to let me know before my departure."

Miles opened his mouth to respond then closed it. She would surely refuse him. Wouldn't she? Uncertainty roiled within him, making him mute.

Blackbourne sighed and shook his head. "Very well then."

"Of course I could have predicted this," Mother said, following her words with a sniff of derision. "Miss Elmsley's reputation has teetered on the brink of ruin since she was presented at court. It was just a matter of time before she showed everyone what she was made of."

Miles turned away from the window in the small sitting room and glared at the woman. How many years had he been listening to her vitriol? Too many. He could not remember a time when his mother had exuded anything but bitterness and negativity. For too long Miles had allowed her to continue, taking on the responsibility of turning things around, bringing her happiness. A task she had rested upon his shoulders since he was a small boy, insisting he fix everything that was wrong with their lives.

And he'd taken up the charge without thinking. Without realizing it was a battle he would never win. A war whose outcome had already been foretold. If he'd had any intelligence at all, after his father's death he would have sent her to one of their properties up north where she could not infect others with her special brand of misery.

He turned back to the window and stared out at the skating pond in the distance, its icy surface gleaming in the sunlight. "I concede, Mother."

"I beg your pardon?"

"I concede." The words came out on a weary breath. He turned once more to face her. "Nothing I do will change anything. I could marry the most esteemed lady in the country, whose every word and deed and movement were the height of propriety and still, you would find fault. It would not be enough. You would continue to be miserable and ornery and mired in unhappiness because that is just your way."

His mother stared at him, her normally pinched mouth going slack. "How dare you say—"

"How dare you assume to judge Miss Elmsley," Miles said, cutting her off. He could not stand to hear another word from her. Not one. "She is the most uncanny of individuals who has had the good sense to realize happiness cannot be found in proper manners and correct behaviors. That it is found in the minutiae. In a smile. A gesture. A kiss."

His mother gasped and her hand reached for the pearls encircling her neck. Red stained her cheeks, giving her usual pallor a hint of color that did little to flatter it.

"Perhaps if you had employed even a modicum of her attitude in your own behaviors, you might have found a sliver of peace over the years. Though, to be honest, I think you prefer your misery. I think you wrap it around you like a cloak of righteousness. Sometimes I wonder if you were always this way, or if it was Father's doing that made you this way. Regardless, it no longer matters."

Miles crossed the room to stand next to where his mother sat staring up at him as if she no longer recognized him. Perhaps she didn't. Perhaps she never had. He'd never been more than a means to an end for her, after all. How odd to think that Marcus had a lifetime of warm regard for the mother he'd had but for a few short years, yet in a lifetime with his mother, Miles could not muster even the slightest happy thought.

"I love Miss Elmsley, Mother. I love her with a depth I had not thought myself capable of. You think her unworthy, but the truth of the matter is that it is I who will never measure up to her. She is a wonder, though likely I have made it impossible for her to hold me in even the most meager of regard."

"This is ridiculous!" Mother shot up out of her chair, her hands fisted at her sides. "I will not tolerate this kind of sideways talk. Have you lost your mind? Or has spending the past weeks surrounded by the loose morals of the lords and ladies present weakened your resolve to do what is right?"

He could not deny living among the lords and ladies that populated Sheridan Park had opened his eyes and made him see life from a different perspective.

"No, Mother," he said, with a smile. "It has not weakened my resolve in the least. If anything, it has strengthened it. Their example has made me see that there is more to life than trying to outrun a scandal not of my making. That allowing a dead man's actions color my future is no way to live. And so I remain resolved to do what is right, but I am afraid I must inform you that my perspective on what is right has changed dramatically."

"Whatever are you saying? Have you taken leave of your senses?"

"On the contrary, Mother. I have never been clearer. I have arranged for a carriage to convey you home."

"To London?" She appeared pleased at this, at least as pleased as he'd ever known her to look. He was almost sorry to disappoint her.

"No, to Bantleford." The family estate where his mother had spent her childhood had remained empty for years, save for the staff who kept the property up as if someone would arrive any day to fill its hallways. Now someone would.

"Are you...you dare to banish me?"

"You have always enjoyed your time at Bantleford and now you may do so full-time. You are no longer welcome in my home. I will provide for you and you will never go without, but I cannot consign the woman I marry to your constant disapproval. She deserves better than that. As do I. Good-bye, Mother."

Miles turned on his heel and walked from the room, the weight he'd carried upon his shoulders for more years than he could count lifting, shrugged off by actions he should have employed long ago.

But better late than never.

CHAPTER THIRTEEN

Insanity, that's what this was.

Pure, unadulterated, potentially disastrous insanity.

If standing outside Patience's bedroom door in the middle of the night, wearing nothing but his nightshirt and dressing grown, did not prove this, he didn't know what did.

For once, his mother was right. He had taken leave of his senses.

His heart pounded in his chest as if the mightiest blacksmith wielded the hammer and he could barely breathe from the impact. Still, he could not help but believe when Charlie told him Patience had left Havelock to discuss wedding details with their cousin, Judith, at Sheridan Park, it was fate telling him to take the chance.

Besides, what did he have to lose?

Everything.

His dignity. His reputation.

If caught, the scandal would be a hundred times worse than the kiss Mr. Farthing stole. Patience would be ruined forever and not even marriage would save her. And his hope of avoiding comparison to his father would be over forever as well.

He was totally out of his element.

What was he thinking? He was still too high on his victory of sending his Mother out of his life to think clearly. He should return to his own room and forget this foolish scheme. One he had concocted after too much brandy.

But the idea of a future without Patience, of her marrying a man she did not love and giving up everything she believed to save a reputation she had nothing to do in ruining was wrong. So wrong and unfair that Miles felt it down deep in his bones.

And his heart.

He could not allow her to do this.

Nor could he willingly give her up to another without a fight.

Bloody hell.

Miles took a fortifying breath and turned the doorknob as quietly as possible, opening the door only enough to slip through and close it silently behind him. Then he froze. Patience stood at the window, her back to him, with the curtain pulled back so that the moonlight bathed her in its soft glow. He leaned his back against the door and soaked up the beauty before him.

"If you have come to try once more to convince me not to marry Mr. Farthing, Judith, you should save your breath. Unless I wish to become a scandal-ridden spinster, it is my only option."

Her words settled around him, the resigned texture they carried a stark contrast to the lively tone he had become accustomed to.

"Is it?"

Patience whipped around at the sound of his voice, a gasp echoing around her. "What are you— ?" She looked down at herself, dressed only in a thin shift that the moonlight easily penetrated, outlining her gentle curves and mesmerizing Miles so well he almost forgot what he had asked, or why he was here. Or what his name was.

God help him, but she was utterly and completely enchanting and every good intention he had flew south with burning intent.

Patience wrapped her arms across her breasts then dropped one hand to cover the shadow at the juncture of her thighs. "What are you doing here? I am not dressed. This is highly, highly improper!"

A laugh burst out of him at the strange dichotomy that she should be the one to say that to him. "I know."

"Then why are you here?"

She had yet to move away from the window and the moonlight kissing the curve of her hips proved most distracting, not to mention the hardening of his member that appeared to have rendered his brain useless.

"Miles?"

"I came here to save you."

Her hands fell away to rest at her sides—Saints preserve him!—and she took a step forward. "Save me? From what?"

"From yourself. Or Mr. Farthing."

She took another step. "Well, which is it?"

Miles rubbed at his temple. Why was it so hard to think? "I can't recall. I had crafted a very articulate argument against this sham of a marriage you've agreed to, but I can't seem to remember any of it at the moment."

"And why is that?"

"I believe you have bewitched me."

"I'm quite certain I haven't."

"I'm equally as certain you have."

"Then we have reached an impasse on this particular matter."

He smiled at her but she did not return the sentiment and his heart lurched in his chest, reminding him of why he had come. To return the smile to her lips. To bring back the infectious laughter that had, only days earlier, come so easily to her. To show her he had seen the error of his ways and that she had been right all along.

"Perhaps you should leave, Miles, before you do something you will forever regret. I will tell no one you were here. Have no fear, your reputation shall remain intact."

She did not understand. "I have already done something I will forever regret."

"Coming to Sheridan Park for the holidays? Yes, I think I share that regret as well."

He shook his head. "No, turning you away at the stables."

Patience clasped her hands in front of her and stared at the floor that separated them. "No, you were right to do so. As you can see, I cannot go long without causing some kind of social calamity. You were smart to step away when you did, so as not to be caught up in it. I know how important your reputation is to you."

Miles released a short laugh and shook his head at her assumption and his own rigid beliefs. How stupid they seemed now. How meaningless. After all this time and all the effort he had put into ensuring no scandal darkened his door, he no longer gave a flying fig. All he cared about was her happiness.

And he could not stand here and watch it slip away, taking with it all the color and life and verve that she had always so embodied.

"Hang my reputation." He pushed away from the door and crossed the space between them until his hands rested upon her arms and he felt the ripple of gooseflesh beneath his touch. "Patience, look at me."

He sensed her hesitation and the release of when she let it go and lifted her head to meet his gaze. The pain and anguish he witnessed in the light blue depth of her eyes cut into his heart, causing a swift, sharp pain that robbed him of breath. He pulled her to him, the only balm he could think of to assuage both their hurt.

The heat of their bodies mingled as one as her arms slid around his waist as if standing here in the middle of her bedchamber barely dressed and holding each other was the most natural thing in the world. The feel of her against him, the rightness of it, created a longing so deep and profound he could find no words to describe it, no way to tell her what it meant to him save for the obvious.

"I fear I have fallen in love with you, Miss Elmsley."

She said nothing at first, then, "Have you?" She did not sound the least bit surprised. He smiled and pressed his lips against the line of her throat.

"Yes. Completely."

"I see. Well…this is quite the conundrum, isn't it, given I have chosen to marry another."

"Reject him. He is not worthy of you." He kissed the hollow of her ear and felt her shiver. Why had he prolonged this for so long?

"And are you? Worthy, that is?"

He lifted his head, reluctant to stop nibbling on her earlobe. He looked at her, disheartened to see she continued to hide her smile beneath the sadness that had swallowed her whole. "No," he admitted. "Not even a little."

"Then why are you here?"

CHAPTER FOURTEEN

Patience's heart that had been beating out of control since the moment Miles's voice had sounded behind her, stilled as she waited. Everything she wished for, everything she could have ever dreamed of wanting hinged on his answer.

Why was he here? She had been so sure of his feelings in the aftermath of witnessing Mr. Farthing's unwanted kiss. Anger. Disappointment. Despite the distance separating them, she'd imagined the downturn of his dark eyebrows, the grim line of his mouth. And when he'd turned away, likely in disgust, she was certain she'd been right.

Yet, here he was in her bedchamber, in his nightshirt and dressing gown with his body pressed against hers, kissing her neck and nibbling her earlobe until she could barely form a coherent thought!

"Are you inebriated?" The question escaped her before he could answer, because truly, what else but severe intoxication would cause the very proper Lord Walkerton who revered his impeccable reputation to do something as scandalous as enter her bedchamber?

He loosened his hold enough to pull her away and look her directly in the eye. "I am not."

She believed him. He was not a very accomplished liar, from her experience. But his answer left her no closer to understanding his behavior than when she had first inquired upon it.

"Then why have you come here? Now? Like this?" Her gaze skirted down the front of him then quickly looked away, too many sinful thoughts crowding into her mind.

"I have come to you now, like this, because I could not wait another moment to do so. I must ask you something and time is of the essence, given Farthing's foolish and self-serving behavior." She glanced away, but his fingers touched beneath her chin and lifted her gaze back to meet his. "You do not deserve to suffer for his actions. Or my inaction."

Tears sprang to her eyes and she feared blinking and causing them to slip down her cheeks, leaving a trail of disappointment and heartbreak in their wake. She did not want Miles to know how badly he had hurt her. After all, he had been right about her inability to avoid scandal in the end.

"Do you want to marry him, Patience? Truly? For if you do, I will leave you now and bid you all happiness. But if you do not, then I wish to offer you an alternative." He took a breath and his hands lifted to her face and held her gently, his thumb brushing away one recalcitrant tear that had escaped despite her best efforts.

"There is no alternative unless I wish to die a spinster of ill repute. I have made my bed, Miles. Now I must lie in it."

"Then lie in it with me."

His words were simple. Short and direct. Yet they made no sense to her. For he could not be asking her what she thought. What she hoped. And so she turned them over in her mind every which way, attempting to arrange them in a way that would make better sense, but nothing worked.

She shook her head. "I don't understand."

"You silly goose," he said with a smile.

And, oh, what a smile. Full and generous and filled with love. But no, this could not be happening. She was the antithesis of everything he claimed to want. So he could not possibly be saying that he wished to—

"Marry me."

She blinked, rendered speechless.

"Patience?"

"Hm?"

"I asked you a question."

Indeed, he had, but obviously the poor man had taken all leave of his senses and as much as Patience wanted to jump at the chance he offered, she could not. For when he regained his sound mind, she would not be able to take seeing the disappointment in his gaze that would tell her he regretted his capricious behavior and wished he had never made the offer.

"You don't want to marry me. You cannot possibly. I am a disaster. A—"

"Then be my disaster."

"You've gone mad, my lord."

"So I've been told, but the truth is that I am mad for you. I love you, Patience. You are a wonder to me. A brilliant, joyous, complicated wonder. I am happy when I am near you. I wish it had not taken me so long to recognize what it was I was feeling and I beg your forgiveness on that account. I can only say in my defense that I have had little experience with love and happiness until you came into my life."

She stared at him, took in the truth of what he said. It was written into every facet of his handsome face. His hazel eyes lit with a delight she had rarely seen before and his smile was unending. He shone from the inside out, as if he had stepped out of the shadows to stand in the light and everything within him was illuminated from within.

"You aren't saying anything."

"I am unsure what to say." What if saying the wrong thing jarred her from this wonderful dream?

"Do you love me, Patience? Even just a little?" She shook her head and the disappointment crowded out the happiness that had been in his eyes only a second before. "I suppose I cannot fault you. I have thwarted your kindnesses toward me at every turn. It is likely nothing more than I deserve—"

"I love you a lot," she said, the words tumbling out in a rush. She took a deep breath. "I love you more than I can express. More than I feel I can hold inside of me without bursting. I love your seriousness and your smile. I love the way your eyes flash when I do something you think is silly and I love how your hair has this way of falling over your brow into your eye and the way you push it back with frustration as if it did so with the sole purpose of irritating you. I love your broken heart and I so desperately wish to fill it with all the love I feel and show you what a wonderful man you are just as you are without having to be perfect. I love—"

But he didn't allow her to finish as his mouth captured the rest of her words and rendered her speechless with the fervor of his kiss, sweeping her up in a passion that ignited with ease and raged with desire. And in that kiss, Patience poured everything she felt for this perfectly imperfect man who she loved so dearly and with such effortlessness. She kissed him to mend the scars left behind by a father's horrible deeds and a cold mother's criticisms and insurmountable expectations. And she kissed him to wash away the fear that he would never be enough.

Because he was. He was more than enough.

He was everything.

He was her everything.

She did not resist when he pushed her shift from her shoulders, slipping the soft linen down the length of her body and exposing her skin to the cool air. And she reveled in the moment when he released her to toss aside his own clothing, leaving them gloriously bare to each other. Stark and uninhibited. She should feel shy. Embarrassed. She did not. Instead, a bold awareness filled her, a courage she had never experienced before.

Nothing in her life had felt more right than this. Than him. Than the two of them together. And oh, how close they had come to missing out on this for the sake of decorum and a misguided sense of propriety. What they were doing was nothing short of scandalous, without a doubt, but if so than let this be the most scandalous Christmas there ever was, for as Miles laid her down upon her bed and covered her with the warmth of his body, she could think of nothing she wanted more.

Until his mouth moved downward, suckling on her breasts and sending spirals of ecstasy shooting through her. Then farther down, where he kissed her most private spot, licking at the sensitive folds and causing her to press her hips into his touch. It was too much. She reached for something she could not see, grasping at his shoulders as if somehow he would know.

And somehow, he did.

He covered her once more, settling between her legs and gathering her in his arms to kiss her slowly and deeply. "You didn't answer me," he whispered as he lifted his lips from hers.

"About?" She pressed against him, receiving a sharp breath as his hardness pushed against her opening.

"Marrying me."

"Oh, that." She arched her hips. Oh, heavens, did a more glorious sensation exist? If so, she might not survive it. "Yes…yes…" Patience pulled at his waist, trying to bring him closer. "Please—"

And he kissed her again, pressed inside, and filled her. She experienced a sharp pain, brief and inconsequential as her body reached beyond it to find the relief she sought. She moved with Miles, watched the pleasure strain against him, the shifting of his muscles as he held himself above her slightly. Patience tried to concentrate, to memorize every second of this blissful experience, but her body would not allow for it. It continued on, rushing forward, racing toward an end she didn't understand beyond knowing she needed it. Then she arrived, toppled over into an abyss with a rush that took over every facet of her being until nothing else existed for a brief, timeless moment. And when the joyous sensation ebbed, left in its wake was the peaceful paradise of being held in Miles's embrace, of feeling his body, depleted and overcome, resting against her.

Patience turned her head and kissed the spot where his cheekbone ended and whispered in his ear. "If you were searching for perfection, my darling, I believe we may have just discovered its whereabouts."

His chest rumbled against her breasts as a quiet laugh escaped him. She would never tire of that sound. He lifted his head and gazed lovingly down at her. Patience reached up and brushed the lock of dark hair that fell upon his brow. "I must agree. Apparently, I should have acted on my thoughts much sooner."

His words shocked her. "Did you think of doing this?"

"Only every day. And every night."

"Lord Walkerton!"

"Shall I give you a sampling of some of the wicked things I imagined doing with you?" He grinned, impish and beautiful. How she looked forward to discovering all the different smiles he had. But then his hand slid down the length of her thigh and his smiles were not the only thing she wished to discover.

"Will I be shocked?"

He lowered his mouth to hover over hers, tantalizing her with the closeness only a breath away. "Oh, I certainly hope so."

And then there was no more time for talk as their bodies took the lead and the love they shared enveloped them in the safety and surety that some gifts deserved to be unwrapped a little earlier than the others.

EPILOGUE

"I cannot imagine a better time for a wedding than during Christmastime," Patience's mother said, dabbing at her eyes with an embroidered handkerchief gifted to her by her daughter only three days previous.

"I have it on good authority," the Dowager Countess of Blackbourne said, glancing across the room at Sir Arran with an expression of utter contentment, "that Christmas weddings come with an extra blessing."

"I can think of no better gift than to see Patience settled and happy," Judith claimed. "A happy marriage is a wonderful thing."

Her husband, Lord Glenmor, lifted his wife's hand to his lips and shot her a glance filled with equal parts heat and love. "Indeed, it is."

"I'm just glad she managed to snag herself a proper husband despite her rather, uh, impetuous nature, shall we call it," Charlie said, his lips twitching with humor, for despite all of his sister's societal missteps, he'd always found her impetuousness his favorite part.

"But how did Lord Blackbourne know to get the special license for the two of them and not she and Mr. Farthing?" Lord Elmsley asked, baffled as he often was by anything that had to do with his daughter.

"I believe you can thank Mr. Bowen for that bit of insight," Lord Hawksmoor answered, though even as he spoke his gaze never left his wife who was huddled in a happy circle with Mrs. Bowen, the two women giggling over something no one dared hazard a guess upon. Though if Hawk were to hazard a guess, and speak it aloud, likely everyone present would turn three shades of red.

He suppressed a wicked grin and excused himself from the group to collect his own bride and perhaps sneak away to a dark corner where he might question her thoroughly as to the topic of their discussions. Provided he could find one unoccupied, given Lord and Lady Huntsleigh had also sneaked away, and Lord and Lady Blackbourne had not been seen for well over an hour despite being the hosts.

Bloody hell, it was a good thing Sheridan Park was a large manor filled with a plethora of dark corners, or likely, they'd all be stumbling over each other. Granted, they could all go to their respective bedchambers, but where was the fun in that?

Sometimes, a little bit of scandal was just the thing to set the tone for a joyous holiday celebration.

"Is it just me," Miles said, pulling his new bride closer until she nestled into his side and tipped her lovely face up to gaze at him. "Or have certain individuals conspicuously disappeared from the festivities?"

Patience smiled up at him and a precious joy filled Miles's chest until his heart was close to bursting with the love he felt for the woman who had brought him such happiness and opened him up to a future he had never dreamed possible.

"It is not you. I spied several couples slipping away. I can only imagine the cause."

He leaned down and dropped a quick kiss upon the tip of her nose, caring little who saw or what they thought. "Perhaps they needed a nap. It has been quite a whirlwind week."

"Indeed, it has, husband."

How he loved that word. Loved it even more when she spoke it, imbuing it with such sweetness. "I find, I too, am feeling the need to lie down for a bit."

Patience stifled a yawn and grin. "I think I may need to join you."

"It would be the height of rudeness to leave our own wedding party. People will talk and I can only imagine the things they will say."

"Well," Patience slid a hand across his stomach and nudged at his neck until every fiber of his body jumped to attention. "If what they say is anywhere near as scandalous as what I wish to do, then they should have much to talk about."

"My dear, Lady Walkerton, such improper suggestions! I am aghast and find I must definitely take a lie down in order to recover myself."

"Shall I assist you to our bedchamber?"

"By all means, yes. I would hate to become lost and accidentally stumble into a dark corner and embarrass one of our friends by interrupting their own little rendezvous."

Patience laughed and whirled about, slipping her hand into his and leading him away from the ballroom and into a future filled with the love and happiness and family he had once thought meant only for others.

Now they were his. She was his.

And he was a very, very happy man.

Dear Readers,

Thank you so much for reading **A MOST SCANDALOUS CHRISTMAS**, Book 8 in the *Sins & Scandals Series*. Miles Radcliffe first joined the series on the periphery, his part that of Lady Rebecca Sheridan's crush. With each book his part grew bigger until I realized he needed a story of his own and heroine who would challenge him to break free of the prison of propriety he had settled into. And who better than the disastrously impulsive Miss Patience Elmsley?

If this is your first introduction to the series, **Book 1: AN INVITATION TO SCANDAL** is currently **FREE** on all digital retailers. I hope you'll check it out and discover where it all began! The series will have 10 books in total once completed. Here is a list of what's currently available & what will be coming out in the near future:

#1 - AN INVITATION TO SCANDAL
#2 - A SCANDALOUS PASSION
#3 – A SINFUL TEMPTATION
#4 - THE LADY'S SINFUL SECRET
#5 - SURRENDER TO SCANDAL
#6 - A SINNER NO MORE
#7 - THE SWEETEST SIN
#8 – A MOST SCANDALOUS CHRISTMAS
#9 – A HINT OF SCANDAL (Spring 2017)
#10 – SINS OF A SOLDIER (TBD)

To keep informed on new releases, check out my **website book page** (http://kellyboyce.com/books/sins-scandal-series/), or sign up for my **Newsletter** at www.kellyboyce.com to keep abreast of breaking news and new releases!

I love to connect with my readers through social media and email and you can find all of my relevant links (Facebook Page, Twitter, Goodreads, Pinterest) on my **website**!

Lastly, in addition to my Regency series, I have also written several **Western Historical romances set in the Old West** and published by Carina Press (**The Outlaw Bride**) and Harlequin Historical (**The Salvation Falls Series**). These are listed on my **website book page** (http://kellyboyce.com/books/salvation-falls-series/) as well.

Again, thank you for reading **A MOST SCANDALOUS CHRISTMAS** and I hope you will consider leaving a review at your favorite online retailer to help others discover **The Sins & Scandals Series!**

Wishing you all the best,

—Kelly

ACKNOWLEDGEMENTS

I am a huge fan of the holidays. Each time they roll around I am filled with a sense of family and possibility. Something I sensed Miles Radcliffe, Lord Walkerton was in dire need of. Apparently I was not alone in this feeling, as several of you emailed to ask me about Miles's story. So thank you, dear Readers, for taking the time to champion Miles's future happiness. I hope you enjoy!

A huge thank you go to my family for their constant encouragement and support. It has been there from the first time I put pen to paper and it continues to this day. You guys are my rock.

To my husband, John – you're like the gift that keeps on giving. Thanks for putting up with the crazy hours I spend in coffee shops banging away on the computer trying to make my characters behave as they should. One day, I promise, there will be a car chase. Love you more and more each day.

And as always, to the group of writers who are always there to support me whether with a sympathetic ear or a kick in the pants – Pamela Callow, Julianne MacLean, Cathryn Fox, Anne MacFarlane, Annette Gallant and Michelle Helliwell. Cheers to you all – you rock!

And as always, my unending gratitude to the wonderful professionals that help me put this book together: My editor, Nancy Cassidy, Kim Killion (cover designer) and Amy Atwell, Author EMS (formatter).

ABOUT THE AUTHOR

Kelly Boyce started writing stories in Grade 2 when her favorite teacher, Mrs. Matheson, showed up with a box filled with plot ideas and she was immediately hooked. But it wasn't until she read Lisa Gregory's *Bitterleaf* that she fell in love with historical romance.

Fast-forward a decade and a bit later whereupon she discovered Romance Writers of America and Romance Writers of Atlantic Canada and learned how to turn those stories, into books and send them out into the big bad world. After that, it was full steam ahead.

A life-long Nova Scotian, Kelly lives near the Atlantic Ocean with her incredibly supportive husband and a clownish golden retriever with a stubborn streak a mile wide.

She loves writing stories about relationships and creating a sense of community around the hero and heroine filled with secondary characters who take on a life of their own.

Her first release, a western historical, **The Outlaw Bride**, was released in 2011 by Carina Press and since then, she has released several more western historical romances with Harlequin Historical: **Salvation in the Rancher's Kiss** and **Salvation in the Sheriff's Arms**, and two Christmas novellas: **The Cowboy of Christmas Past** and **Christmas in Salvation Falls**.

Once she completes her regency series, *THE SINS & SCANDALS SERIES* in 2017, she is contemplating a spin-off series for the Caldwell sisters and also making a foray into contemporary romance and women's fiction.

www.ingramcontent.com/pod-product-compliance
Lightning Source LLC
Chambersburg PA
CBHW030125260626
47156CB00008B/2790